THE CAT STOLE YOUR TOME

GHASTLY GRIMOIRE MYSTERIES BOOK 1

JEANNIE WYCHERLEY

The Cat Stole Your Tome
Ghastly Grimoire Mysteries Book 1
BY
JEANNIE WYCHERLEY

Bark at the Moon Books

Sign up for Jeannie's newsletter:
www.subscribepage.com/JeannieWycherleyWonky

The Cat Stole Your Tome was edited by Christine L Baker

Cover design by Cover Affairs
Formatting by Tammy
Proofreading by Johnny Bon Bon

Please note: This book is set in England in the United Kingdom.
It uses British English spellings and idioms.

The Cat Stole Your Tome is dedicated to the memory of Dr James Thomas formerly of the University of Portsmouth

A true history wizard who taught me so much and changed my life.

James, you'll live on in my memory always

xx JW xx

CHAPTER ONE

"Did you hear the latest?"

I had my head in a fridge. Not my fridge but the fridge at work. I stood up so quickly I nearly crowned myself on the overhanging counter. I needn't have bothered. Jess, the office gossip, wasn't addressing me. She was speaking to Lionel Beechwood, the 'father' of the office, huddled in the corner of the small room waiting patiently for the kettle to boil.

I might have known. There was no love lost between Jess and me. I tried to have as little to do with her as possible.

And, happily, she with me.

On this occasion, however, given the sly, sidelong

glance she sent my way, I had a feeling she wanted me to listen in to the conversation.

"What latest is this?" asked Lionel, almost dutifully, as he poured boiling water over his teabag.

I kind of felt sorry for Lionel. He was a dull, gentle man in his mid to late fifties at a guess. Average height, average looks, average strength spectacles. He'd worked here in the permit section of the Ministry of Witches since leaving school. The longest serving member of the team, he turned up day in, day out, man and boy, wearing his faded, pale-blue Witchy civil service robes and clutching his lunch bag as though it was his most valuable possession. In the three years we'd worked together on the same team I had never known him take a sick day, cheek the managers, bitch about a colleague or leave the all-important lanyard containing his Ministry of Witches pass at home.

Personally, I think that's pretty good going. Especially for a man who had been overlooked for promotion time after time after time.

Jess, who modelled her look on 1950s Hollywood starlets such as a young Marilyn Monroe or Jayne Mansfield, tossed her glamorous blonde curls and widened her already huge eyes, all the better to show off her ridiculously long—they had to be fake—lashes. Never a day went by when I didn't experience feelings of inadequacy in her company—at least in the looks department.

I mean, I'm not Ugly Betty, but I'm no Grace Kelly either.

But them's the breaks, huh?

I ducked my head to continue hunting for the pack of mini pork pies I'd brought in the day before yesterday and not opened. The problem with sharing a work fridge is that snacks have a habit of mysteriously disappearing. Undoubtedly, my pork pies had found a home in someone else's belly.

"I've heard through the grapevine that the powers that be are looking to lay people off," Jess announced.

The powers that be? That would presumably be her boyfriend. Our line manager's line manager. I rolled my eyes at a Babybel at the back of the fridge.

"Is that so?" Lionel asked, his tone neutral. I'd never seen him ruffled or even slightly emotional. Occasionally he would smile, sometimes chuckle a little, but he'd soon revert to his calm, quiet, watchful self. His personality was as grey as the trousers he wore beneath his robes. He gently mashed the teabag against the side of his plain cream office mug, barely scraping the sides and not spilling a drop.

"Apparently!" Lionel's lacklustre reaction hadn't dampened Jess's enthusiasm. "Redundancies in all departments! Even among the IT wizards in the basement!"

I gave up on the pork pies—they'd probably be out of date by now anyway—and stood. I'd have to make do with my dried-out cheese sandwich and the bruised apple at the bottom of my bag.

"Oh, hi, Cilla! I didn't see you there," Jess sang.

"Zilla," I corrected her automatically, ignoring the obvious fib. Of course she'd seen me! And to add insult to injury, she managed to get my name wrong every time she deigned to speak to me. I'm sure it's something she does on purpose. I'd learned to simply correct her and not otherwise react. Reaction is what she wanted. To rub me up the wrong way.

But I couldn't be bothered. Not with her, not with any of the office politics. Having worked in various departments for the Ministry of Witches Civil Service since leaving university eight years prior, believe me, I've put up with more than my fair share of office bullying and passive-aggressive line managers.

And I'm totally over it!

So, much like Lionel, I kept myself to myself and my nose to the grindstone and did the job I was paid to do.

And the job I was paid to do?

Issue permits.

Permits for broomsticks—flying them, not owning them. According to Regulation MOW ZZXTBF100089123, subsection 18B, you don't need a permit to own a broomstick, you'll be pleased to hear. In the past, I'd issued permits for exotic familiars. Permits for portal travel. Permits for private detectives. Permits for advanced spellcraft. Permits to open a potionery. Permits for the practice of cosmetic alchemy. The list of permits the Ministry of Witches is responsible for is endless. I won't bore you with them all, but I must have worked in every department and issued every permit possible!

My team—six of us including Lionel, Jess and my line manager, Izo—had, as you will have gathered, specific responsibility for broomsticks. Lately, I must confess, I'd seen a dwindling workload. Fewer witches were using broomsticks—it's an antiquated practice, after all—because in today's world, it's so much easier to drive a car.

Not so easy to park though.

"Worrying, isn't it?" Jess chirruped. She didn't sound worried at all. And why would she? Friends in high places and all that.

Lionel met my eye. "No point worrying about it until there's something official," he said, finally extracting his teabag and disposing of it in the bin.

Again, not a single drip. I was impressed.

I nodded. Rumours of redundancy swept around the building like wildfire three or four times a year. Nothing much ever came of them.

"I think there's more to it this time," Jess said. "Would you mind?" She indicated the fridge and I moved out of her way, preparing to take my boring cheese sarnie back to my desk. *Lunch at my desk. Woo-wee! It's an exciting life I lead.*

"You *think* there's more to it or you *know*?" I asked, then mentally kicked myself. *Don't sound interested and don't get involved, you peanut!*

Jess shrugged and pulled a Tupperware lunch box out of the fridge. "I have my sources."

We all know about your sources, I thought.

She popped the top off her box. It had compartments! Each compartment had something in it. Carrot sticks, celery sticks, baby tomatoes, olives and hummus by the look of it. Yummy. My lunch paled in comparison.

Maybe I should make more effort.

With my lunch.

Not with Jess.

"Time will tell," said Lionel. He looked pointedly at Jess. "Could you pass the milk?" he asked.

"Oh, ummm, yes!" Jess hurriedly popped a carrot stick in her mouth and reached for the milk.

"Catch you later," I said, and left them to it.

Back in the office, I dropped into my wheelie chair, deposited my sandwich on the desk and rummaged around on the floor for my bag. I tend to use a daysack rather than a handbag because I can fit everything I need in there. Along with a load of stuff I don't, of course. At any one time I had a book or two on the go, usually one fiction and one non-fiction, and there would be magazines too. I rummaged among the lip balms and hand sanitiser and tissues, a notepad, a coin purse, my wallet, an old lanyard, one half of a pair of mittens, a brolly and ... *Where's that blooming apple?*

"Hey!" Sally, the lady who occupied the desk directly opposite me and another member of our team, popped her head above the divider. "Zilla?"

"Mmm?" I glanced up, shaking my hand free of a tatty grey tissue.

"Did you see the email?"

"Which email?" I asked. I'd already dealt with about sixty of the blasted things so far this morning. "You'll have to be more specific."

"From Jo Burke."

The head of human resources. "No."

"It came about five minutes ago."

I'm on lunch, I thought. *I don't have to deal with anything at least until I've finished my grotty sandwich!*

"It's from upstairs."

"Upstairs?" I pricked my ears at this. Upstairs where HR and the managers lived? Did this mean Jess's rumour was true?

"They've called us to a meeting at four." Sally grimaced.

"Oh," I said. This didn't indicate good news. I nudged the mouse on my desk, waking up the monitor. It had helpfully logged me out.

Lionel dropped into his seat across the aisle. I peered over at him, wondering whether to say anything, but he had swung his chair around to face the wall and was already reaching for his newspaper. Every lunchtime was the same. He made himself a cup of tea, he ate his sandwich—like mine, it was never anything particularly exciting—and he would do the crossword in *The Celestine Times*.

I decided not to bother him. Thirty minutes for lunch was the most relaxed part of his day. What right did anyone have to encroach on that?

And anyway, what had he said in the kitchen?

Time will tell.

CHAPTER TWO

Four o'clock rolled around. The broomsticks team and the exotic familiars team were directed into the same meeting room on the second-from-top floor of the Ministry of Witches building. This is where human resources and some of the upper civil service managers lived. I think the original idea was that all of the offices on this floor would be paperless, with everything digitally encoded, and the walls kept pristine and white—but we're talking about witches and wizards here, so of course, chaos reigned. Gradually, posters had appeared on the scuffed walls, and the posh carpets had become stained—both from coffee spillages and the tears of lesser employees—so the whole floor had a lived-in feel. This, despite the fact that few of us mere—paranormal—mortals ever came up here.

Unusually, coffee and biscuits had been laid on for the meeting. "They must be trying to sweeten us up," muttered Sally as she grabbed a couple of the chocolate digestives and took a seat between me and Lionel. I smooshed up a bit because the table would normally hold a dozen maximum, but the exotic familiars team numbered eight in total and ours was six. Also in attendance was Jo Burke, the sour-faced HR director with hair that looked like it had been sucked through an aeroplane's engine, and her smilier second-in-command, Kesandra Miggs. Next to Kesandra, perching on a seat like a little bird and poised with a notebook and pencil, was a young woman I had no prior knowledge of. I noticed she was a nail-biter.

My line manager's manager, Gibahn Hagen, scurried into the room as though he was rushing between appointments and was struggling to fit us in, a haggard expression on his absurdly handsome face. I stole a quick look at Jess—Gibahn was rumoured to be her lover, after all—but she was fiddling with a ring on her right hand. The blue of the sapphire matched the colour of her eyes.

"Are we all here?" Gibahn asked, peering around the room.

"Well I am," announced one of the members of the exotic familiars team. Robin, I think his name was. Fancied himself as a bit of a wag.

"All here from broomsticks," Izo, my boss, said.

Gibahn nodded briskly. "Thanks, Izo. Evanora?"

Evanora, team leader for exotics, allowed her myopic gaze to sweep the room before confirming. "Yes."

"Excellent. Let's make a start." Gibahn didn't bother with a chair—he would have been hard-pushed to insert himself around the table anyway. He cleared his throat. "As you may already know, the whole of the Civil Service is facing funding issues, and unfortunately that includes the permits department."

A number of people shifted uncomfortably. *Here it comes*, I thought.

"The entire service has been asked to find ways and means to plug the shortfall, and I'm afraid"—Gibahn glanced nervously around—"we're looking at a twenty per cent reduction in staffing."

Silence.

Eventually Robin piped up, "Twenty per cent?"

He laughed, although in disbelief rather than humour. "How does that work when you're a member of a team of eight?"

"For the purposes of this exercise—"

*Exercise? He's calling this an **exercise**?* I reached for a chocolate-covered finger.

"I'm having to make the cuts across all the teams I'm responsible for."

"Across all the permits teams?" Evanora sought clarification.

"That's correct," said Gibahn.

I crunched my biscuit. The room was oddly still. My munching sounded impossibly loud. Izo blinked at me.

"So ... how many ...?" Evanora asked.

Gibahn exchanged a look with Jo. She pursed her lips. "I have one hundred and nine people on my teams," Gibahn said "I've been asked to reallocate twenty-two of them."

Pandemonium broke out. A few chairs were pushed back, there was a flurry of mumbled curses—although not of the hexing kind, you'll be glad to hear—among the rising crescendo of agitated voices. I swivelled my head to the right. Lionel remained still, his face giving nothing away. Evanora had turned pale.

"Guys, guys!" Gibahn raised his hands, palms up, appealing for peace. "Let's get through everything we need to and then you can have your say."

More shuffling greeted this, along with murmurings of discontent.

"Reallocate them?" someone from the other team asked. I didn't know his name, although I recognised him.

"There will be natural wastage of the usual kind ... you know, people moving between other teams in the service, people retiring, people choosing to leave of their own accord—"

"But probably not twenty-two of them," the same man said, his voice snide.

"We have accepted that we'll have to let some people go." Gibahn winced, looking thoroughly miserable.

Izo's head swivelled, taking in everyone on the broomsticks team. I had a feeling he was trying to appear sympathetic, but given he wasn't long out of nappies—a fast-track graduate, don't you know—and had ridiculously little genuine experience of life, he couldn't quite pull off this 'I'm one of you' expression.

"I'm assuming that these figures include team

leaders?" Evanora asked, more shell-shocked than anyone else.

Jo nodded an emphatic yes. Gibahn reluctantly confirmed that. "I'm afraid so."

Izo's eyebrows shot upwards and he pulled at the collar of his robes.

Now Jo took the floor. "We will be able to offer a few remuneration packages, but specific criteria will have to be met for anyone who wishes to avail themselves of redundancy."

"Such as?" Sally asked.

"It depends on a number of factors, mostly to do with how many we lose through natural wastage and how we reallocate jobs. It may be that certain skills will no longer be required—"

I tuned out for a moment. The details didn't really matter, did they? I wouldn't be volunteering to go anywhere. The Civil Service was all I knew. It was my only form of income. I'd be trying to keep my job.

But as it turned out, there was more bad news.

"The service has decided to amalgamate the broomsticks and the exotics teams," Jo was saying.

"Seriously?" Robin asked. "We don't have much in common."

Sally snorted. "Oh, please."

I suppressed a smirk, sympathetic to her reaction. The problem with the exotics team was that they had an overinflated sense of their own self-worth. Anyone can answer the phone and fill in a form—you don't have to possess expert knowledge of alligators, peacocks or snow leopards. However, I didn't want to draw attention to myself so I kept my mouth shut. I hate public speaking.

"How are you going to decide who stays and who goes?" Sally asked.

Gibahn harrumphed. *That's a terrible case of frog-in-the-throat-itis you have there*, I thought. "We decided it will only be fair if everyone reapplies for the jobs available."

There was a collective gasp of dismay. I confess, this time, even I may have huffed out loud in despair. I'm truly rotten at job interviews!

"Better start updating our CVs, everyone," said Robin, surveying his competition.

Lionel picked that moment to push his chair back and stand. Deathly pale, he looked as though he was about to address the room—maybe make a pitch for one of the available jobs—but he flushed, two pops of bright pink on his cheeks. "Would you excuse me?" he asked, and, with some difficulty, edged around the circle of chairs and left without another word.

After that, the meeting turned into a bit of a free-for-all, with some attendees speaking passionately and others, like me and Jess, remaining mute. I was glad when the less-than-merry gathering came to a swift end, just after half past four.

As much as I'd like to have headed straight home, I didn't think clocking out early would be a good look, not when I would soon be job-seeking, so I returned to my desk, logged back into my computer and began answering emails.

To my surprise, Lionel hadn't returned to the office. His lunch bag sat on his desk, and his computer monitor was on, although not logged in.

Clock-watching until the minute hand dragged its sorry backside around to the twelve, I was up and out of my chair so quickly when it finally did that I tripped on an electric cable and sent my mouse flying. Izo, huddled with Jess, arched an eyebrow my way, looking pointedly at the clock. *It's home time, mate!* I thought, but I kept my face neutral. I had to make my way past him to reach the door. I nodded at them as I strolled by.

He turned back to Jess. "I can't believe I'm going

to be reapplying for my job so soon! I only just started!"

At least your CV will be up to date, I thought. *You've only been here five minutes! Mine's going to need a proper overhaul.*

Jess mumbled something incoherent and vaguely supportive. She could afford to be magnanimous. I couldn't see Gibahn getting rid of her. "Do you think Evanora is a better line manager than me?" Izo asked her.

The kitchen cockroach is a better line manager than you, I thought, but then I was out of earshot and didn't catch Jess's response.

Clear of them, I practically sprinted down six flights of stairs, swung through the revolving doors in the lobby and burst out into the square. Damp air greeted me; the paving stones were wet and the trees in the square glistened with drops of water. It had rained recently—hard—and now the air was fragranced with petrichor, one of my most favourite smells in the world.

I paused and inhaled deeply. *Mmmm.* As I let my breath go free, my gaze alighted on a lone man sitting on a damp bench.

Lionel.

Oh. Had he been out here all this time? It was unlike him to be the first to leave the office.

I glanced about. Maybe someone else would come out and think to check on him. People were streaming out of the building behind me, but no other members of my team, so far as I could see.

Perhaps Lionel wouldn't want to be disturbed.

I began to walk away.

And then I couldn't. I didn't have it in me. I *had* to check on him.

I retraced my steps and edged alongside him, peering down at his slumped shoulders, his dropped head.

"Lionel?"

He started, as though he'd been miles away.

"Sorry," I said. "I didn't mean to scare you. You didn't come back after the ... meeting." I gestured towards the Ministry of Witches. Was it my imagination or were Lionel's eyes glistening? A little red-rimmed?

He cleared his throat but didn't say anything.

"Sorry." I apologised again. Something I seem to spend my life doing. "I didn't mean to intrude." I offered a tight-lipped, self-deprecating smile and stepped away.

"It's fine," he said, and I paused. "I'm fine."

Liar, liar, pants on fire, I thought. "You don't look fine," I said, and that was bold of me, I admit.

He sniffed. It was a snotty sniff. The sort of sniff men do when they've had a bit of a cry. That single sound convinced me. I took a seat beside him. "You don't have to talk to me," I told him. "I know we barely know each other"—*even though we've been working together for three years*—"and maybe that's my fault more than yours. I don't tend to mix so well at work." I laughed. "Or anywhere, really. But"—I pointed at the nearest tree—"we can talk about other things if you like. Maybe how many birds are nesting in that tree? I can't see any nests though, can you?" When he didn't reply, I hurried on, "I don't even know what kind of tree it is, do you? That's terrible, isn't it? Not even being able to identify a tree!" I shifted uncomfortably. The damp of the bench was penetrating my robes. "Crikey, Lionel. Couldn't you have found a dry seat to sit on?"

He laughed, a proper belly laugh.

Now it was my turn to be startled. "*Are* you okay?" I asked him. It felt like the right time.

"I envy you," he said. "You're such a great people person."

I confess to being taken aback by this. "I am?" *I'm definitely not.*

"I hear you talking on the phone to customers all the time, and you have such an easy way about you."

"Oh," I said. "Thank you." I would never have thought this about myself. "I suppose it's easier when you're not face to face," I admitted. "I sometimes find people in the flesh a little overwhelming. But besides, *you're* great too."

"Professional," he said. "Experienced." He said this with an element of bitterness. "You have a natural, easy charm. I'm sure you'll have no problem retaining your job."

We were getting to the crux of the matter. "Are you ... Are you worried you won't?" I asked, carefully. I didn't want to make him cry again.

He sniffed once more. "I'm the oldest member of the team by far. The most expensive to employ. I should imagine if they have the choice, they'll put me out to pasture. And then what? Who's going to offer me a job at my age?"

He had a point. Jobs were hard to come by in the current economic climate. Unless you wanted to work in a coffee shop on minimum wage and a zero-hours contract. However ... we should remain positive. Right? "But as you said," I reminded him, "you're *experienced*. The most experienced person on the entire permit floor! Gibahn *needs* you on the team. He'd be a fool to let you go."

"You're very kind," Lionel said. He pulled something out of his pocket and began to play with it. It looked like a coin. I watched him in silence for a while.

Eventually he asked, "Do you enjoy your work?"

"Yes." It was an automatic response. I didn't even think about it. Of course, the moment I said yes, I reconsidered my answer. "Kind of."

He waited.

"Well ..." I was struggling now. "Put it this way, it's a job."

He smiled and nodded.

"It pays the bills." *And other well-known cliches*, I thought. "Hmmm."

"What did you want to do with your life?" Lionel asked. It occurred to me we had never had a conversation of this length before. After this, would we default to ignoring each other in the office?

"I studied literature at university," I said. "I'm not sure what I planned to do with that. I just like reading. When I graduated I looked for a job—any job—that would pay enough to cover my rent and my bookshop hauls. And that's how I ended up here."

Lionel chuckled. "But you haven't always been in broomsticks?"

"No, I worked in a few departments before this one."

"What you need is a job that has something to do with books," Lionel said, twisting the coin between his fingers.

"Like what? I'd need more qualifications to become a librarian. I can't afford to go back to university."

"Publishing?" Lionel suggested.

"It's a bit of a young woman's game. Plus, y'know, Oxbridge ..." I shrugged. "You need contacts. I have none." Spits of water began to strike my face. It was about rain again. "Besides! Why are we talking about me?" I patted his arm. "I was trying to cheer *you* up!"

He smiled at me. A genuine, warm smile. It lit up his features, made him seem somehow less beige and boring.

"Listen," I said, jumping off the damp bench and swinging my daysack around so I could rummage inside for my battered old brolly. "If it's any help at all, I'm happy to look over your CV and make some suggestions on how to update it. We can bring all your experience and wealth of skills and knowledge to the fore." I winked at him. "You'll give Jess a run for her job!"

He tossed his head back and guffawed. I couldn't quite get over this transformation in him.

"Email it over to me," I told him. "My personal email is zilla dot chaplin at witchmail dot com. It's an easy one to remember. Have a great evening!" I sidled backwards, wanting to put my brolly up and escape the rain.

"You too," said Lionel. "And thank you."

"My pleasure." I smiled, waved and strolled away. I'd managed to cover ten or so yards when I heard Lionel calling to me. When I turned back, he was standing, facing me.

"What about a bookshop?" he asked. "If you like books, you could run a bookshop?"

I nodded enthusiastically and clamped a hand over my heart. "You know, I would love that. It would be a dream come true. But I'd need capital, and I have none. None at all! I don't even own my own flat—" I grimaced.

Lionel walked towards me. As he reached me, he held up the coin in his hand. "I want you to have this."

I studied it. Up close, I could see it was no ordinary coin. Hexagonal-shaped, it had a hole in the centre. More of a token than a coin.

"A long time ago, an old witch gave this to me. She said that one day I would meet someone who would need good luck more than I—"

"Lionel—" I tried to interrupt.

"No," he said, his voice firm. "Hear me out. She said if I held onto it until that day and I willingly gifted it to that person, good luck would come to the beneficiary but also to me."

I frowned, considering this.

"I feel like we could both do with some luck right about now," he said. "So I want you to have it."

"Okay," I said, not wholly convinced. How long had the token sat in his pocket? How would he feel without it?

"There is a catch," he said.

Uh oh, here we go. "Is there?"

"Yes. One day you *must* give it up in the same manner that you received it."

"I see," I said. I didn't imagine for a moment that this would be too difficult.

"If you agree, it's yours," he said, and flipped the coin high into the air.

I watched it rise. Up. Up. Then fall in slow motion, spinning all the way, heads over tails over heads over tails, the rain—like tiny prisms—sparkling around it.

I reached out and caught it in my right hand, wrapping my fingers tightly around it. Perhaps it was my imagination, but it seemed to shiver with its own inherent energy.

"I agree," I said.

CHAPTER THREE

Shaking the rain from my umbrella, I stepped into the lobby of City View Court. City View was a misnomer if ever there was one because the only view was of the main road out the front and a similar-sized block across from us—a group of eight one-bedroom flats. I'd lived here on the first floor since leaving university and had been lucky. Rents in the area were soaring but mine had remained vaguely affordable.

It wouldn't be if I lost my job though.

I checked for post, something I automatically did every time I entered or left the building. The landlord or property owner or someone, way back in the 1960s when these flats had been built, had created a wooden bench with lids that lifted up rather like old-fashioned school desks. There had once been a key so you could keep things secure, but for ease—for parcels and free newspapers and so on—most tenants didn't bother with these. You could post things through the letterbox-type slit or you could simply lift the lid and drop things in before slamming the lid back down, much like our postie did.

Not that there was ever anything much in mine except circulars and bills or an occasional postcard from my great-uncle Claudius, my late grandmother's brother, who suffered with a bad case of wanderlust. Apart from Claudius, I'd often wondered whether anyone ever writes cards and letters anymore.

Today was different.

A parcel had been left on top of the post boxes. It half covered my lid, so I needed to move it in order to check for mail. Holding the parcel in my left hand, I opened the lid with my brolly hand, shaking droplets everywhere. *Oops*. Nothing inside though. Surprise, surprise.

It seemed odd that the parcel had been deposited on top. The boxes were plenty big enough for small packages, and this one was about the size of an A4 folder. Wrapped in brown paper, it had been secured with well-knotted string. I turned it over, expecting to find a name and address so I could slot it into the correct box, but there wasn't one.

Peculiar.

I was about to replace it where I'd found it when something inserted itself between my ankles. I jumped a mile.

"Miaow."

A cat.

"Hey, kitty," I said, pulling a face. I'm not a cat person. Don't get me wrong, I like them. They're cute. From a distance. But up close—

"Waaaachoooo!"

—they make me sneeze.

"Bless you."

"Thank you." My response was automatic. I looked around, expecting to see one of my neighbours standing somewhere nearby, but nobody was immediately apparent. I peered up through the gaps in the stairwell, but I couldn't see anyone up there either.

The cat continued curling between my legs. I must confess I was quite taken with it. It was fluffy and an unusual bluey grey, with a flash of white on its chest and a white right front paw.

How do cats keep their feet so clean?

"Waaaahchooo!" My head nearly dislodged from

my shoulders, so violent was my sneeze. That was enough for me. I blinked, my eyes suddenly maddeningly itchy. "Excuse me," I said, snuffling. Hurriedly abandoning the parcel in the same place I'd found it, I extracted myself from the cat's caresses before rushing headlong upstairs, my nose beginning to stream.

"Ugh! Why do cats do this to me?" I grumbled, fumbling for my keys and letting myself into my flat. Throwing myself inside the bathroom, I dumped my umbrella in the shower and quickly ran a basin of water. As soon as it was full, I dunked my face before rushing to wash my hands thoroughly, to help ease my reaction to the cat. That done, but still sniffling, I yanked my robes off and flung them towards the linen basket. My work trousers and shirt quickly followed.

"Freedom!" I bellowed and headed into my bedroom to find a tissue to blow my nose with and something scruffy to wear. Friday night and I had a date with the laundry and some housework. It doesn't sound exciting but of course, the greater the number of chores you manage to complete on a Friday night, the more opportunity you have to laze around on Saturday, and to my mind—given the height of my to-be-read pile—this could only be a good thing.

First things first. I stuffed a load of washing—mixed colours, I'm single, I can't be precious—into the yawing jaws of my old Hotpoint machine, added a bright green Faery pod and slammed the door shut. I don't mess around. Everything on 30 or 40 degrees for an hour. Job's a good'n.

Next, I put the kettle on. Tidying up and dusting goes faster when accompanied by a mug of builder's tea. It's thirsty work, after all. Unfortunately, a survey of the fridge revealed the horror that is ... a lack of milk.

"Urgh!"

Rats! I'd meant to go shopping on my way home, but the encounter with Lionel had ousted that intention completely from my mind. I glared at the empty shelves. It would be necessary to do a full shop in the morning—there went my lie-in—but I needed something for this evening, and I seriously couldn't live without milk for my tea and coffee.

Grimacing, I reached for my parka. It was too warm to wear it, but it had the advantage of a hood so I wouldn't have to rescue my umbrella from the shower. After locating a shopping bag, my purse and keys, I slipped on my boots and yanked open the front door.

The blue cat was sitting on the thin handrail where the balustrade from upstairs curved round and down. Cats have impressive balance—I mean, that's no mean feat. It stared at me with wide, hypnotic, yellow eyes.

"Back, Satan," I said and edged around it, leaving as much room as possible, before scampering down the stairs, dashing back out into the drizzle and racing for the nearest corner shop.

When I returned, maybe twenty minutes later, the cat had thankfully disappeared. *Probably wise,* I thought, wondering which of my neighbours had adopted the rotten thing. The landlord forbade all creatures—the great and the small—from sharing our habitations, and that included familiars of all persuasions.

However, the parcel that had originally been sitting on the mailboxes now rested on the thick coir mat outside my door.

"Huh." I paused, water dripping into a shallow puddle at my feet, studying the plain packaging once more, waiting for it to reveal who it belonged to.

Needless to say, it didn't.

Sighing, I leaned over and scooped it up, then, juggling a bag full of groceries, my keys and the parcel, I navigated the deadlock and swung through into my flat. Once inside, I slammed the door, determined never to venture outside again.

Or at least until Monday rolled around and I had to go back to work and fight for my job ...

Hmm.

Okay. Never to venture outside *until* tomorrow morning, when I'd have to shop for the week.

I deposited my bag of groceries on the counter and stared down at the parcel in my hand. No matter how much I frowned at it, it failed to sprout an address.

"How do I know it's for me?" I asked aloud. "How do I know it's not a bomb or something?"

Because who would want to bomb you? my inner sceptic replied.

"You never know!"

I dropped the parcel next to the groceries, took off my outdoor robes, hung them up and set about doing chores. I checked on the washing machine first —nearly done—then popped a frozen ready meal into the oven. While the washer hummed away to itself and the oven ticked, I zipped around the flat and tidied. I say tidied. I basically stacked everything into piles to be sorted at a later date. I grabbed a black bag and dashed around, emptying the contents of wastepaper baskets from the living room and bedroom into it before depositing it by the kitchen bin, a reminder to take all the rubbish out next time I set foot outside. I swept the kitchen floor, cleared the week's clutter from the surfaces, washed up and finally wiped down the counter and the cabinets.

The washing machine began its final spin. Noisy at the best of times, on this occasion the sudden clanking nearly gave me a heart attack. "What the —!" I crouched down beside the porthole window, expecting to see an anvil or something of similar size and density being thrown around in the drum alongside my smalls, but there was nothing immediately obvious.

Then it dawned on me. Lionel's token.

Oops.

I should have taken a bit more care of it than that!

"I clean forgot," I murmured as the machine finally completed its cycle. I watched as the load trundled through its final moments, the drum rocking back and forth and loosening all my garments, then it stopped, buzzed and beeped. A long minute later, the safety lock clicked off. I hurriedly opened the door and yanked out my Ministry of Witches robes, patting down the pocket until I found what I was looking for. There it was. The token. Not harmed in any way. Just a little bit shinier.

Relieved, I placed it down on the counter next to the parcel. The oven was counting down its last few minutes until supper could be served, so I took a moment to study the parcel one more time. The string that secured it had been tied in an elaborate knot. Intrigued, I pondered on whether the knot had been deliberate or whether it had simply ended up that way. It was unlike anything I'd seen before. I plucked at the string with the tip of my index finger, allowing my imagination full reign. *Could the knot be* ***enchanted****?* I remembered classes from way back, when I was in school, where we'd learned about charms and spells that could be utilised to tie objects up in specific ways for a myriad of reasons. Secrecy had been the primary one. You could enchant the string or knot, and anyone who attempted to undo it would receive a hex.

"All the more reason not to open it," I muttered,

pulling open my cutlery drawer to rescue a sharp knife.

I stared down at the knife in my hand. What was I doing?

Perhaps ...

Perhaps I meant to have the knife handy so that I could slit the plastic covering on my meal as it came out of the oven.

Perhaps ...

Instead, what I did next changed my life forever.

CHAPTER FOUR

There was no *poof*!

No explosion of stars and smoke.

Instead, the string fell away and the parcel seemed to breathe out, loosening the paper, making itself comfortable, the way I might after removing tight jeans.

Cautiously, I slipped a finger under one edge of the brown paper and pushed it aside. Beneath the wrapping was a book of some description, which I might have guessed from the shape of the parcel in the first place.

So far, so good. As you may have already gathered, I'm a sucker for books. Perhaps someone had gifted me one. Fully curious now, I unwrapped it completely, pushing the paper aside.

Hmm.

Now that I could see it, it didn't look promising. Approximately nine by seven inches or thereabouts, it had a stiff, plain cover in a mucky light brown. Slightly stained. *Water? Oil?* I turned it over. The spine was half an inch, if that, and broken in several places. There were no other markings.

I flipped the cover. It fell open easily. Nothing on the first page. Flicking through the rest of the book, I frowned. Nothing on any page. A blank book! A blank, well-thumbed, *old* book with a broken spine and empty pages?

"Well, you're a mystery," I said, just as the timer on the oven beeped.

Dinnertime.

I arranged a glass of water, my congealed cheesy pasta something-or-other in a bowl, and an apple—fresher than the one I'd eaten at lunchtime—on a tray, meaning to head into the living room and leave the notebook or journal—or whatever it was—on the counter. But I couldn't do it. I'd only managed a few steps and changed my mind. I perched the book on the side of the tray and took it with me. Settling myself on the couch, I turned on the telly and ate mechanically, but my eye kept returning to the book.

Curiosity had the better of me. I didn't bother finishing the pasta—it was grotty anyway—I simply turned down the volume on the television and reached for the book again.

Now, I'm not an idiot. Both of my parents are witches from a long line of witches. My younger brother and I attended a school for witches and wizards. There, I learned some magick and then progressed to the London University of Magick and Witchcraft, where I learned a little more in my first year before concentrating solely on literature—of both the paranormal and the mundane variety.

I instinctively understood that what I had here was an enchanted book of some description. It would need unlocking. Unfortunately, I didn't have the first clue how to do that. Pushing aside my tray and abandoning my apple altogether, I positioned the book face up—or what I assumed was face up—on my coffee table and studied it.

Somewhere, lost in the far reaches of my memory, was a university session I'd had with one of my favourite lecturers, Dr James Thomas. He'd taken us to an archive hidden in the depths of the Ministry of Witches library in Celestial Street, where numerous ancient tomes had been kept locked away, some in glass cabinets, some in sealed caskets. The archivist who'd curated the collection—his name escapes me—had informed us that the books were often sent in anonymously, and sometimes they arrived completely blank but laden with magick. He had a team of experts he could call upon, if he needed to, who could unlock the secrets held on the pages, but oftentimes the books were stored under lock and key and nobody interfered with them.

Back at the university, good old Dr Thomas had shown us a basic 'reveal' spell we could use on old documents. It was a classic case of 'here's one I prepared earlier' as he handed around thin note-books and invited us to discover the message he'd left within.

My message had said, *It might take a year, it might take a day, but what's meant to be will always find a way.*

Of course, I was still waiting to find out what was meant to be in my case. Ho hum.

I thought back to that lecture. How had we done it? I didn't recall finding it difficult. I jumped up and scampered through to the kitchen, eager now. All I needed was salt. Back then we'd probably used black salt or green salt or pink salt or something, but at the end of the day, salt is salt and the rest is your imagination. I grasped a container of sea salt from the back of the cupboard, then decided against it. Maybe all salts are not equal, after all. What if sea salt was too powerful? What if I unleashed an ocean or tsunami or something in my living room? To be on the safe side I opted instead for the ordinary, bog-standard, tiny-grain, everyday salt you'd put on your chips.

Back in the living room, I seized the nearest candle—sage and woodsmoke scented—a box of matches and some incense and rummaged in a drawer for a chunk of coal and my Ministry of Witches Civil Service wand. Standard issue. Nothing to write home about. Arranging the items in a vague circle and incorporating my glass of water, I figured I'd covered all bases.

Good.

Sitting cross-legged next to the coffee table, I lit the candle and the incense and began to empty my mind and slow my breathing. Deep, deep, deep, calming breaths. *Mmm.*

"Gracious ancestors," I murmured. "I call upon you today to guide my practice." I curled my lip. "It's been a while, I know. You may well have forgotten who I am. I haven't had much need of you for a while"—ten years, in fact—"but if you wouldn't mind dusting yourselves down ..."

This conjured a comical image to my mind and I almost laughed, but then I remembered I was trying to be serious, so turned the giggle into a cough. The auld folk would never notice.

"Just out of interest ..." I continued, indicating the plain book before me and wafting the incense away from my face. "Is this an enchanted book? If it is, please can you help reveal who it belongs to? I'd like to find its rightful owner."

I smoothed the cover and carefully flipped the book open before sprinkling a healthy dash of salt all over the inside page. Then I turned my hands palms up, closed my eyes and meditated a few moments more before calling up a surge of energy from deep within my core. "*Reveal*," I whispered. "Who do I return you to?"

Opening my eyes, I gazed down at the book. The page remained disappointingly and obstinately blank.

"Meh," I said. "Thanks for that."

Dismissing the ancestors—if they'd ever *actually* been there; maybe they *had* abandoned me and gone off in search of a distant cousin more adept in the use of magick than I—I dashed some of the salt away from the page in a fit of petulance.

The paper shimmered where I'd touched it. "Ooh!"

I lightly stroked the paper once more, watching as a streak of colour—a dark beige—spread across the page. I pitter-pattered my fingertips on the surface. Small puddles of brown formed. Staring in fascination, I watched as half a dozen shades of brown rippled outwards and met their neighbours. The colours fought each other, creating shapes and shadows until at last they took on a sharper edge and merged and danced and became curling lines that twirled and twisted and finally ...

Began to form letters.

I held my breath.

The letters tangled among themselves, shifted, melted and reformed to reveal ... a name.

"Murgatroyde Plunge," I read aloud. Sitting back, I regarded the television. It was still on, but muted. "What an odd name." I repeated it. "Murgatroyde Plunge."

It was a start, but I needed more clues. Lightly brushing the rest of the salt away, I searched for other marks. I could make out some faint drawings. Green leaves? Yes. Carefully crafted in coloured pencils. The outline of a foxglove? A dash of pink and magenta. A smear of brightest yellow and a smudge of charcoal. A bumble bee?

The sudden enormity of what I'd done sent a jolt through me. I'd released one of this book's secrets. This was the first magick I'd performed in nearly a decade. That in itself was crazy ... but additionally, I had the jarring sensation of being caught looking at something intensely private. *I'm not this book's owner*, I reminded myself. *This isn't intended for my eyes ...*

Suddenly alarmed, I flipped the cover closed and pressed my hands down hard on the book's surface, as though this would retract what I'd done. Leaning over, I blew out the candle and wafted at the resulting smoke. Where I'd removed my hand from the cover, a blue smudge remained. Frowning, I lifted my other hand. The warmth of my palms had revealed part of the original cover. Instead of the card of the cover as I'd first known it, now I was looking at stiff leather, a deep, distressed, green-tinged blue, layered at the edge with a pattern of ivy or some other climber, and with the curve of an oval towards the middle.

Intrigued, I returned my palms to other parts of the cover, pressing down as I had before but, whether it was because my hands were cooler or because I'd broken the spell, I failed to reveal any more.

I shouldn't be doing this, I reminded myself. *This belongs to Murgatroyde Plunge. I should try to find her and give it back.*

But where would I even start to look for her?

CHAPTER FIVE

I awoke the next morning to the sound of rain lashing against my window. "Fine," I mumbled, nestled deep beneath the covers. "I'm not going anywhere anyway." But you know what it's like. The moment your body realises your brain is conscious again, you have a pressing urge to pee. It therefore turned out I was going somewhere after all. Down the hall to the bathroom.

Blinking back sleep, I stared into the mirror above the basin at my tousled hair. *There's no hope*, I told myself, washing my hands and debating whether to try to go back to sleep or write a shopping list while brewing the first pot of tea of the day.

As the wind buffeted the window panes, I decided a pot of tea and my Kindle might be just what the doctor had ordered. Gracious! I'd even bought some chocolate biscuits during my foray into the corner shop the previous day! The perfect Saturday morning treat.

As I moved back into the hallway, I heard a scratching at the door. In my half-awake state I couldn't imagine what it would be, so I approached the door, slid back the chain and bolt and cracked it open.

Quick as a flash, something whisked past my bare ankles.

"Oi!" I spun around in alarm, but whatever it was had disappeared. Taking a moment, I replayed what I'd seen. Something small. Bluey grey. And hadn't that been fur that had rubbed against my skin?

"Hu-hu-hu—" My nose began to run. "Hu-hu-hu —" My eyes began to water. "Hu-hu-hu-hu-CHOO!"

That blasted cat!

Grumbling, I plodded into the kitchen, scanning the corners and the worktops. Not in here. "Hu-hu-CHOO!"

The living room? Glowering, I stomped down the hall. There were plenty of hiding places in here. Behind the sofa? Under the table or the sideboard? On top of the bookcase?

No joy. It wasn't here.

"You'd better not be in my bedroom!" I shouted. I really didn't fancy having to strip the bed and try to get everything dry on a day as wet as this one!

Unfortunately, I found the cat sitting calmly on my bedside table. On Murgatroyde Plunge's book.

"What do you think you're doing?" I hissed. "You can't be in here. I have ha-ha-ha-allergies! Wah-tchoo!"

The cat regarded me somewhat balefully. It had remarkably yellow eyes. Is that a thing in cats? I thought they all had green eyes. I'm not sure I'd been this close to one in, like, forever!

"Go on! You have to go! Go! Go!" I flapped at it. Ineffectually, as it turned out. It remained obstinately where it was. I sneezed rapidly three times in succession, each time more vociferously than the last. "Urgh!" I moaned. "You hab no idea what you're doing to be." I sat on the bed, rummaging under my pillow for a tissue, massaging the bridge of my nose, trying to alleviate the stuffiness. Tissue found, I blew hard, trumpeting like an elephant, loud enough to wake the street.

The cat's eyes followed my every movement. Then it stood, raised its tail and blinked. Ordinarily, I wouldn't have commented on the blink, but it was so deliberate and so obviously aimed at me that I couldn't miss it.

Then it sneezed in sympathy with me. A cute little cat sneeze. Perhaps it had an allergy to humans.

Almost immediately the stuffy sensation in my sinuses eased. I sneezed another couple of times, but my eyes had stopped itching and watering. A good face wash and I'd feel almost normal, I reckoned.

I stared at the cat. The cat stared back at me.

"Did you do that?" I asked.

It didn't answer. I mean, why would it? Cats don't talk, right? "No, of course you didn't," I answered for it. "It must be last night's antihistamine kicking in." Would a tablet have lasted that long? It seemed unlikely to me, but what other explanation was there?

"You can't stay," I told the cat. "I may not be snotting all over the place now, but that doesn't infer that you and I have any sort of relationship. You don't belong here. Somewhere, someone is looking for you."

I tried to shoo the cat off the bedside table again, without touching it. It refused to budge.

"I can't feed you or home you or stroke you or play with you or do anything with you," I said. "I don't want to be taking allergy tablets twice a day for the rest of my life. You have no idea—"

The cat yawned.

It yawned!

It had the temerity to break into *my* house—after a fashion—enter my bedroom without so much as a by-your-leave, take up residence next to my bed and *yawn* at me!

"Quite frankly, I'm insulted," I told it. "You could show a little more consternation at being thrown out." I wondered if I dared poke it or something? Would it bite me? Scratch me? That's a thing cats do, isn't it? My finger hovered near its shoulder while I considered my options. While I was thinking, it arched its back and nuzzled into my fingers.

I jerked my hand away in horror. "Don't do that!"

If a cat could roll its eyes, I think this one would have done.

I hesitated. Its fur was so soft. Unable to resist, I tentatively reached more and scratched between its ears. It seemed to like that. When I didn't resume sneezing or snuffling, I relaxed into petting it a little more. "I wonder what your name is. Not that it's any of my business." I ran my fingers gently around its ears. "And besides ... you have to go home, so I refuse to properly acknowledge your existence."

I gently pushed it. "Any chance you can move? Only you're sitting on someone else's property and I daren't damage it because I have to return it."

The cat didn't budge.

"Look, you're going to have to leave at some stage! I need a cup of tea and I want to get back into bed—"

The cat nestled down into a crouching position. That told me all I needed to know.

Sighing, I abandoned it where it was and trooped out to the kitchen. While waiting for the kettle to boil I gave my hands a good scrub, just in case the cat's fur decided to belatedly cause me issues. Bizarrely, it didn't feel like it was going to though.

I picked up the packet of antihistamines, wondering if they were extra strong and had lasted overnight, but they seemed to be the same ones I normally purchased. "Maybe I'm less allergic than I thought I was."

Tea—and biscuits—secured, I ambled back to the bedroom. The cat remained exactly where I'd left it, and that presented me with something of a problem because I needed space to place my tea.

Lifting my mug, I showed the cat the steam. "You'll have to move. This is hot—"

I didn't finish my sentence. The cat hopped gracefully from the bedside table to the bed and proceeded to nest where my feet would normally be. "Don't go making yourself comfortable," I sniped, noting the rattle of my blind as the wind buffeted against the window. "It's not that I want to chuck you out—well, I do, just not in this weather—but—"

I stopped. Where the cat's rump had been sitting on Murgatroyde Plunge's notebook, it had heated it up, revealing more of the cover. "Have you got a magickal backside?" I asked, carefully placing my mug of tea on a coaster and reaching for the notebook. The central oval had now been revealed, although there was no image inside it and more of the embossed ivy had been exposed. Was it my imagination or was the notebook thicker and heavier than the previous day? I flipped the cover, staring at the facing page.

"Who *are* you, Murgatroyde Plunge?" I asked, tracing her name with my fingertips. The page had revealed its full glory now. Pretty scribblings and curlicues, flowers and bees. There was no contact information, however.

I began turning pages, thick with age. Surely

they hadn't been this way yesterday? Perhaps my memory was failing me. The next few pages contained shadows and grainy outlines, bolder marks that indicated writing ... but none of it was legible. It was almost as though the book was reawakening after a long sleep and dragging memories from the deep past.

"Miaow."

The cat was standing by the bedroom door. I hadn't noticed it jump off the bed. As soon as I looked its way, it stalked off into the hallway, tail high. Tucking Murgatroyde's book under my arm, I followed it to the front door.

"You're leaving?" I asked, arching an eyebrow.

The cat craned its neck, staring up at me. "*Miaow.*"

"Oh." Opening the door, I watched it mince its way out onto the landing then, with a flick of its fluffy tail—it had a white tip, I noticed—it leapt gracefully out of sight.

Go home, strange little thing, I thought, and hurried back to my bed and my rapidly cooling tea.

CHAPTER SIX

"Hi!"

In an effort to locate either Murgatroyde Plunge or someone who knew something about the parcel being left on top of the mailboxes downstairs, I'd tapped on a few doors in my block. Given that I'd lived here for eight or so years, I had surprisingly scant knowledge about my neighbours. People had come and gone over the years—some I'd been glad to see the back of, and some I'd missed, but I'd never made any proper friends here.

The lady who lived in the flat on the ground floor—Gita was her name—was from somewhere in South Asia. Her flat *always* smelled of spices. Every time she opened the front door she flooded the communal areas with the scents of her homeland. It made me yearn for places I'd never seen. *Mmmm, heavenly*! She didn't speak an awful lot of English, but she smiled a lot. When I showed her the book and its wrappings, she shrugged and disappeared inside. A few moments later she returned with a Tupperware box full of samosas for me and a tub of some kind of sauce. She nodded happily and closed her door, leaving me standing there none the wiser about whether she recognised the book but richer for the encounter.

The old couple in Flat 2 must have been out because there was no answer from them, and the flat directly across from me was currently empty so, after leaving the samosas and sauce in my kitchen, I climbed the steps and tapped on the door of number 5. At first there was no reply, and I was about to turn away when I heard the chain being pulled back. The door cracked open and half a pale face—with smeared eyeliner and black lipstick—glared out at me.

"Hi," I repeated when she didn't respond. "I'm Zilla from number three—"

"Babe, I know who you are," she growled. "What do you want?"

Taken aback, I stammered an apology. "I'm sorry to have disturbed you—"

"It's fine." She sighed and opened the door a little more. I realised she was wearing a sleep shirt. I must have woken her. "I haven't been in long."

"I'm really sorry—"

"Whatever." She shrugged. She shot words like bullets. "Babe? What can I help you with? If it's to do with the rubbish, I had loads and I had to use your bin—"

"No, I'm not here to complain about anything. I just wondered if you recognised this?" I held up the book, half wrapped in brown paper.

She squinted at it. "Should I?"

"Not necessarily." Her aggression was making me anxious. I took a step away. "It turned up at my door and I don't think it's meant for me—"

"Who did it say it was for?" She reached out and took the book from me, dropping the paper.

"There was no name on the outer wrapping," I told her, bending over to retrieve it.

"It says Murgatroode Plug here." She pointed to the name inside the cover.

I carefully folded the paper. "Murgatroyde Plunge. Do you know who that is?"

"Nope," she said, thrusting the book back towards me. "Is that it?"

"Yes. Tha—"

"Good. I'm going back to bed." With that, she shut the door. It didn't slam, but let's just say it closed *firmly*.

This weekend was already more people-y than I wanted it to be, and it was only Saturday morning.

"Phew." Taking a breath, I smoothed down the book as though its feathers had been ruffled by the encounter with number 5 as much as mine were.

"Murgatroyde Plunge, you say?"

I spun around. Mr Redhill at number 6 regarded me with interest. He was a sweet old chap. A bit hunched over. He must have been well into his eighties, and yet he still managed the stairs without any problems. I regularly saw him coming and going, although I don't know where from and to—he obviously had an altogether better social life than me.

"Yes." I lifted the book to show him. "Do you know her? Or him?"

"Her." He smiled and squinted at me. "I haven't heard that name for a long, long time. What is it you have there?"

"I'm not sure." I moved closer so he could see. "I mean, it's a book, with her name inside, but other than that, I can't say."

"Come in for a moment," he said. "Let me find my spectacles."

I made a great show of wiping my feet on his mat, even though I was wearing slippers and I hadn't actually been outside. It seemed polite to do so. He led me through his hallway and into his living room. The layout of his flat was the same as mine, but he'd done far more with it than me. Where I had plain walls, his were covered with a dark-wine-coloured, textured paper. His lampshades—on the ceiling and floor lamps—matched perfectly. He had a three-piece suite in a rich azure blue with gold throw cushions, and a rug that drew all the colours together. Jazz played on his stereo. Vinyl, I noted. Actual *records.* The overall effect was warm, sophisticated and cosy.

"Where did I leave them?" he asked, patting his pockets. "In the kitchen, perhaps. Can I offer you tea?"

"I'm fine, thanks," I told him. He nodded and disappeared, giving me a moment to check out the numerous framed photographs on his walls. In pride of place were some larger images of him with someone I assumed might have been his wife. I was much taken with a sepia-toned image of a younger Mr Redhill wearing unusual ritualistic robes of some description.

"I cut a fine figure there, didn't I?" Mr Redhill snorted when he caught me looking.

"You certainly did. What was the occasion?"

"I'd been working as a diplomat in Japan. I was about to leave and they wanted to present me with a ceremonial sword."

"Ah." I could see it now. The stylised robes did look Japanese. "You look magnificent."

He smiled. "My wife thought so too." He drew my attention to a portrait of them together, taken perhaps when they were both in their fifties.

"She's pretty," I told him. She did have a soft prettiness about her. Sympathetic eyes. A gentle smile.

"Glynis. She was beautiful." He sighed. "Been gone fifteen years. It seems like five minutes some days, and other days it feels like a lifetime."

"I'm sorry," I said.

"Never be sorry," he told me. "I expect you say that far too much."

Unsure what to say, I opened my mouth and closed it again, frowning.

"I'm good at reading people," he told me. "That's the art of being a diplomat. You pay extra attention to details." He tapped his nose.

"Is that so?" I asked.

This time his grin was enthusiastic. "It is!" Rubbing his hands together, he said, "I know your name is Zilla Chaplin because I've seen it on your mailbox. I know you work at the Ministry of Witches because I recognise the robes you wear—"

"They *are* a bit of a giveaway," I agreed.

"I would assume you have a degree and that you've been working in a dull job for some time."

I smiled. There was no skill to this. These days you had to have a degree to work in our Civil Service and, let's face facts, weren't all jobs at the Ministry of Witches as dull as ditchwater? I would say so.

"And therein lies your problem," he said.

"That I have a dull job?" I asked.

"That you assume all jobs in the Civil Service are dull."

Had he read my mind? I frowned. "But they probably are."

"Undoubtedly," he told me. "Therefore, you should find something else."

Am I really having this conversation less than twenty-four hours after having the same one with Lionel? It's like some giant conspiracy.

He indicated his dining table. "Let's have a look at your book, shall we?"

For a moment, distracted by the conversation, I'd

forgotten why I was here. I shook myself and hustled over to the table, but had to wait for him to clear off a load of clutter: mainly newspapers, magazines and books, but also candles, a couple of silver goblets and a sizable crystal ball.

He spotted me ogling it. "It belonged to Glynis," he told me. "She was an amateur prophesier and fortune teller. Picked those skills up as a teenager. I'm nowhere near as accurate as she was but I like to have a go now and then; it helps me to feel closer to her."

"That's nice," I said and placed the book on the square of table he'd cleared.

Mr Redhill slipped his spectacles on and leaned over to take a better look.

"It's enchanted," I said, probably unnecessarily. He could see for himself that part of the cover had yet to be revealed.

"Hmm," he said, turning the cover over using the tip of his finger and revealing the faded flowers and the curly writing on the front page. "Well, well, well," he muttered. "Murgatroyde Plunge as I live and breathe." He looked sideways at me. "How did you come by this?"

"That's the weird thing," I replied, feeling guilty all over again. "The parcel was left on top of my mailbox downstairs. Partly on mine and partly on number four's, but there was no name or address on it so I left it there. I wasn't expecting anything. Then I found it on the doormat outside my flat."

"Peculiar. Suggests someone wanted you to have it."

"You think?" I was glad to hear him say that. At least it sounded as though he didn't disapprove that I'd opened the package. "Obviously it isn't mine, so now I want to return it if I can."

He arched a scruffy eyebrow. "You might have your work cut out there."

My heart sank. "Why do you say that?"

He indicated I take a seat at the table. I did so. He sat beside me, flicking through the pages of the book. They looked to me as if they were becoming increasingly dry, like old parchment.

"I'm surprised you've never heard of her," he said, "but perhaps it's a generational thing. Time passes. The old folk choose not to remember, so the memory isn't passed down ..."

I frowned. "Choose not to remember what?"

"I hate to speak ill of the dead—"

I did a double take. "She's dead?"

Mr Redhill blinked in surprise. "I don't know. I shouldn't have said that. I'm making an assumption."

"Based on?"

He took a breath. "Based on ... I suppose because she would be old—*very* old—if she were alive."

"Fair enough." I couldn't argue with that. "How old is very old?" I'd known of witches and wizards reaching some particularly grand ages.

"Older than me, and I'm ninety-two."

"Ninety-two?" *Crikey!* "Wow, congratulations. That's a grand age. You're looking good on it, Mr Redhill."

He snuffled, slightly bashfully. "I try. It's been more difficult since Glynis passed away."

"This Murgatroyde person may be alive though?" I asked.

"Indeed. But"—Mr Redhill lightly tapped the book—"why would she give up her grimoire if she was? I've never known a witch willingly do that."

I stared down at the book. It hadn't occurred to me that this might be a grimoire. "Am I being an idiot?" I asked. "How do you know this is her grimoire?"

Mr Redhill returned to the title page where Murgatroyde Plunge had so flamboyantly written her name. He flipped a page and pointed at the scratches and lines that had taken shape there. At first I couldn't see what he was referring to, but then, as my eyes focused and tried to make sense of what they were seeing, I distinguished the words 'instructions' and 'spell' and 'tincture' handwritten in a black pencil, alongside a partial, smudged drawing of an evil eye talisman.

"Ah." Mr Redhill was right. You would never expect a living witch to give up her grimoire. All those years of experience, wisdom and experimentation locked into one dog-eared volume. A grimoire was often the most precious of a witch's belongings.

Besides their familiar, of course.

That thought pulled me up short. "There was a cat," I said.

Mr Redhill waited for me to explain.

"I didn't link the cat with the parcel, but now that I think about it, perhaps they were together." I thought back to my first encounter with the cat. That had definitely coincided with finding the parcel. But —pffft!—what was I thinking? Cats can't carry parcels. "It's probably not related ..."

Mr Redhill shrugged. "And yet your instinct is to assume it may well be." He laughed. "There's no such thing as coincidence, Zilla."

I was pretty sure there was, but I didn't want to contradict him, so I smiled politely. "What can you tell me about Murgatroyde Plunge?" I asked. "Perhaps I can trace her family?"

"I doubt she had a family."

"Why do you say that?" I asked.

"Because she spent a good proportion of her life in prison."

Oh! That came out of nowhere! "Prison? What did she do to warrant going to prison?" I asked.

Mr Redhill shook his head and closed the book with a slap. Pushing it back to me, he said, "It was a long time ago. I don't remember."

That was a lie. "But—" I started to protest.

Mr Redhill jumped in. "If I were you, I'd take this book and burn it. No-one will be interested in the contents."

"But—"

"Burn it!" Mr Redhill urged me, his faded blue eyes burrowing into my soul. "Burn it to ashes!"

CHAPTER SEVEN

Back in my flat, I sat by the window staring at the rain, Murgatroyde Plunge's grimoire resting in my lap and chaotic thoughts playing bumper cars in my brain.

So many questions!

Why had Mr Redhill been so loathe to discuss Murgatroyde's history? He'd been interested enough to call me into his flat to look at the book, but once he knew what it was, he'd zipped up faster than a goblin in a sleeping bag on a snowy night on Snowdon.

What crime had Murgatroyde committed that was so awful Mr Redhill didn't wish to talk about it?

But most of all, why had the grimoire turned up on my doorstep?

I had half a dozen books sitting on my coffee

table demanding my attention. That had been my sole plan this weekend. Read books, drink tea, eat biscuits. Rest up, ready for a week of snide gossip and mundane misery in the office as we all geared up to reapply for our jobs.

Sighing, I turned my back on the books and reached for my laptop instead, flipping it open and waiting for the home screen to load. I scanned my emails—nothing from Lionel, but the weekend was still young—then pulled up Ghoulgle.

Murgatroyde Plunge, I typed.

There were a couple of results from WinkedIn and Witchbook, but the links further down the page interested me most. These old news stories, rehashed in the poorer quality papers, were twenty or so years old and archived for future posterity. I clicked on one and was immediately besieged by adverts. I hastily shut it down. Life is too short. I tried another one. The same thing happened. Huffing in annoyance, I tried a third site—and this time, *bingo*!

Where is Murgatroyde Plunge now? screamed the headline.

Okay, it didn't actually scream, but it was written in big blocky black letters, so it might as well have.

Those of us with long memories and unforgiving hearts will never have forgotten Murgatroyde Plunge.

The 72-year-old witch was recently freed on life licence from Witchwood Scrubbs after serving forty-five years. In 1958, the notorious child killer was sentenced to life for the abduction and murder of eleven-year-old Greta Mayflower and her seven-year-old brother, Socrates. Greta's body has never been recovered.

Goodness, I thought, pressing my hand over my heart.

Good witch gone bad, ran the subheadline.

Born in 1931, Murgatroyde Plunge excelled academically and creatively. After attending the Paranormal College of Art, she trained as a teacher and was employed at Hecate's Primary School, east of Celestial Street. She was, by all accounts, popular and well thought of by her colleagues, pupils and parents alike.

The Mayflower children were reported missing after they failed to return to their foster home on 20th March 1958. A search was launched immediately.

Police enquiries found that while Greta had waited at the school gates, Socrates had stayed behind to talk to Plunge about a model aircraft he was building. Plunge claimed that she offered him some advice. The children left the school grounds. This would be the last time they were seen alive together.

Socrates' body was found dumped in a burial place in Tumble Town close to Pillinger's Art Products and Craft Store, often frequented by Plunge. Interviewed by The Celestine Times *later, the owner claimed that the teacher had accompanied the children to the shop to buy a specific brand of newfangled acrylic paint.*

Plunge was charged with the abduction and murder of the two children after the police concluded she had lured them to the art shop under false pretences and strangled the seven-year-old boy after he became belligerent and demanded to return home.

After a trial lasting just eight days, Plunge was found unanimously guilty by a jury of her peers.

I frowned. "I hope the police had more to go on than the fact that Socrates was behaving like a brat."

Where is Plunge now? the paper asked.

"Yes, do tell," I muttered.

Plunge, who has always maintained her innocence and has therefore never revealed the whereabouts of Greta Mayflower's body, was released under licence into the care of the local probation service. She was recently spotted visiting a supermarket in Cheapside.

The paper ran a photo of a haggard-looking woman with long, curling grey hair and a dour expression. She had her arms wrapped around her chest and her head down as though she was aware she was being stalked by the paparazzi but was no willing participant.

I stared at the image, curious to put a face to the name. This was the owner of the grimoire? I reached for the book and flipped the cover. The inside page had now completely revealed itself: the delicate, life-like flowers, the curling ivy, the wings on the bee. The colours were warm and bright. I breathed out in appreciation and watched as blades of grass rippled over the paper and the fronds of a dandelion exploded into the air. Tiny seeds like umbrellas scattered across the right-hand page. Smiling, I turned the page and watched as the seeds floated on the shadowy blankness before settling and taking root where they landed.

Within moments, green shoots emerged and reached up towards me beginning the cycle of life all over again.

I glanced back at the screen on my laptop and scrolled up to the top. The article dated from March 2003. Over twenty years ago! Mr Redhill had imagined she must be dead, and that seemed reasonable. I quickly totted up the figures. If the reporting was accurate—and with this rag, who could tell? —*and* if

Murgatroyde Plunge was still alive, she'd be well into her nineties by now.

Feasibly, she *could* be alive.

I did another Ghoulgle search for 'Murgatroyde Plunge obituary', but nothing came up.

"That doesn't mean anything." I pushed the laptop away and slumped. "She might have died in obscurity ..." Was that even possible these days? Didn't everything have to be notified to the relevant authorities? And wouldn't it have been of 'media interest'? *Ugh.*

"What do I know?" I muttered. "I know nothing."

Except that was a lie. I knew a lot more than I had done a few hours ago. I knew Murgatroyde had served time for killing children. A lot of time. And deservedly so.

Something buzzed near my ear and I flapped at it.

*Deservedly so ... **if** she did it.*

From my vantage point well over sixty years later, the evidence appeared flimsy. Not circumstantial, perhaps, but tenuous enough to cast doubt on her conviction. There would have been little, if any, forensic testing available in the 1950s. The court would have relied on esteemed experts—gentlemen of a certain age who made the right vowel sounds and dined with the right people at the right gentlemen's clubs.

"Come on, Zilla!" I rubbed my forehead. "You're talking as though there was a conspiracy against her."

The buzzing grew louder and I turned my head, annoyed that some flying insect had invaded my space. It was a bee. I hesitate to say it was *the* bee from the grimoire, but the fluffy orange on its jacket seemed to suggest it was. And yes, you may think I'm deluded, but I swear the dandelions had grown up out of the pages and were waving in a non-existent breeze beside me.

I reached out to touch one, the bright yellow of the petals fresh and dewy. This was magick as I'd never experienced it. I could smell fresh grass and the moist scent of the soil. As my fingers brushed a dandelion, the flowers drooped and sank into the page. In moments, all that was left was a drawing of a dandelion meadow and the black outline of the seed umbrellas floating across the paper.

I turned a page. As before, this one was blank, but dark shadows played at the edges. The seeds scattered across the surface, the soft skeletal shape of each merging with creases in the paper, forming lines, more sketches. I watched entranced as a structure of some kind took shape. Straight lines, wonky lines. A building. Part brick, part wattle and daub. A big window. Too big to be a house ...

A shop!

An invisible pencil filled in shadows and sketched smaller objects. Items in a window. But the window was made up of square panes of glass, and it was difficult to tell what they were. Then a sign began to appear above that window. Even before the proprietor's name had been revealed, I knew without doubt what I was looking at.

Pillinger's.

The Art Products and Craft Store.

Hadn't that been the shop close to the burial place where the body of Socrates Mayflower had been discovered?

A thrill emanated from my core and rippled through me, the hairs on the back of my neck prickling.

Was it possible that Pillinger's shop still existed? If it did, I could find it and from there visit the burial place.

But what was I thinking? If I was expecting to find evidence in a long-forgotten murder case to support my idiotic notion that Murgatroyde Plunge had been innocent of the crime for which she had been convicted, then I was truly grasping at straws.

"I need to give my head a wobble," I whispered, staring out of the window at the relentless rain. "Who in their right mind would go out on a day like today?"

But I couldn't quell my rising excitement.

My mind was made up.

"I would. That's who."

CHAPTER EIGHT

Huddled into my robes, the hood pulled out across my brow in an effort to prevent the teeming rain from getting in my eyes, I stood beneath a five-way direction sign and observed the double frontage of Pillinger's art and craft shop.

I'd sacrificed my old, cheap brolly to the bin gods after it had turned inside out and completely given up the fight as I hurried along Celestial Street looking for the turning into Cross Lane. Just as well. The lanes and pathways around Tumble Town were something else, a complete tangle of tiny streets winding this way and that, most of them no wider than five or six feet, some noticeably less. I hadn't ventured here for years and I didn't know my way around at all. It would be easy to become hopelessly lost. For a while, I'd found myself reconsidering my motives.

All my life, I'd lived in and around Celestial Street, much like every other witch and wizard I knew. Despite the name, Celestial Street is *not* a street—although it might have started out that way over a thousand years ago—but a wider area, like a small town, I suppose. It contains its fair share of affluent addresses, as well as smaller homes for the 'ordinary' mortals amongst us. At the top of Celestial Street, you would find the main Ministry of Witches building with its domed roof and clock tower, alongside various other ministries and civil service buildings and the entrance to the underground station. The university, the courts and other municipal necessities were also dotted around here. Celestial Street *itself*, the main thoroughfare, was lined with dozens and dozens of quirky shops and some larger stores such as Herod's. At the opposite end to all of the Ministry of Witches buildings, you'd find the cheaper retailers.

But if you wanted dirt cheap, or rare or unusual or—dare I say it—illegal or banned items, then Tumble Town was where you headed.

Tumble Town is best described as an enclave for paranormal beings who simply don't belong in Celestial Street. It's a place for miscreants and ne'er-do-wells, for thieves and robbers, for misfits and murderers. A place where people go to disappear. It's where the blackest of our kind hide: dark mages, sages, warlocks and evil sorcerers. Having said that, while it's not somewhere you'd choose to venture for a fun day out, some of the best potioners and magicians were said to live here, hidden in the labyrinth of streets that spread all the way down to the Thames at Deadman's Wharf.

The population of Tumble Town, at a rough guess, must easily outnumber that of Celestial Street by about four to one. Maybe more. There had been several attempts to take a census, but they had come to nought. Given the number of humans living in such a limited space, you can imagine that the houses and dwellings were on the small side. In the oldest parts of town they were squeezed together so that the second storey bulged out into the street, meaning that many of the houses leaned out above your head, and daylight was a rare commodity. From what I could see today, the gas lamps were burning perpetually, shining mute yellow light into dark corners, largely ineffectually.

Probably the most disturbing aspect of Tumble Town is that the shadows teem with life. Wherever you go, whatever you do, it feels as though someone is watching you. The deeper I'd ventured down Cross Lane, the more certain I'd become that ghosts were following me because I could distinctly hear whispering and laughing—mischievous or snide—whenever I paused to get my bearings.

Goblins maybe? Or pixies?

Something worse?

I'd peer around, scan the shadows, but there was never anyone there.

I shivered and kept a tight grip on my bag.

Pillinger's was open for business. It had crossed my mind that I could arrive here to find the shop boarded up, but the lights were on and someone was moving around inside. I'd also noticed that many of the businesses in Tumble Town didn't open until midday, some even later, probably to cater for the nocturnal proclivities of the population. Celestial Street operated on extended 'mundane' hours—meaning businesses and offices would open at eight, half past or nine, but they also stayed open until three or four in the morning. Here in Tumble Town, opening hours extended until dawn.

Pillinger's window contained a wide variety of colourful goodies: pens, pencils, paint sets, brushes, easels, model kits, embroidery kits, a spinning stand with hundreds of skeins of silk thread, piles of felt, teeny wooden mannequins with movable limbs, bottles of glue and so on and so forth. Remembering the striking colours of the meadow in Murgatroyde's grimoire, I couldn't help but wonder what brand of paints and pencils she'd used.

A woman, head wrapped in a woollen shawl, scuffled past me. Although she didn't look directly my way, I could sense her wonder. I realised my behaviour probably warranted scrutiny. Nowhere in Tumble Town did you ever see anyone overtly staring at anyone or anything else. People tended to mind their own business.

I definitely approved of that.

A gust of wind, heading up Cross Lane, hit me full in the face. I blinked the rain from my eyes. I could smell the river.

What are you doing here? You must be mad. What are you hoping to achieve by loitering around a shop where a child murderer once bought supplies? Go home and put the kettle on!

I half turned away, but something in my solar plexus squeezed itself in disappointment. *You're so close to an adventure*, my mind seemed to say.

I don't want an adventure, I argued with myself. *I want to sprawl on my sofa and read a book!* But unfortunately, something inside me, deeply curious, had other ideas.

Blast!

Making my mind up, I pivoted and dashed across the streets that formed the crossroads before I could change my mind. Gripping the door handle, I pulled, pushed and finally burst through into the dry.

"Good afternoon." A young woman with dreadlocks arranged in a bun on top of her head nodded at me from behind the counter.

"Afternoon," I replied, feeling slightly self-conscious. What on earth did I think I was going to do here? This woman was my age, nowhere near old enough to know about the events from the 1950s.

"Are you looking for anything in particular?" she asked.

"Erm ... just mooching," I said, kicking myself. I made a show of admiring the embroidery silks. Truth to tell, apart from a brief few months when I'd been into cross-stitch, I'd never tried my hand at embroidery. I didn't have much talent in that department.

I do like to draw though. I moved on to the art materials.

The young woman slid out from behind the counter to shelve some paintbrushes. I cast a little side-eye her way. She caught me looking and I flushed. "I like your hair," I said.

"Oh, thank you." She smiled. "Saves on hairdressers."

"Ha!" I fiddled with a lock of my own damp hair, hanging in a rat's tail, and wondered how I'd look with a hairstyle as cool as hers. What would they say at work? Did it matter? Would I even have work to go to in a few weeks? Hmmm. Well, okay. If they made me redundant, maybe I'd dye my hair bright green and wear it in dreadlocks.

That sounded like a plan. I snickered quietly.

"Can I help you find anything?" the young woman enquired again.

Wouldn't it have been lovely to ask whether she had any information about a historic murder case? I didn't have the nerve to come straight out and ask. "Erm ... I like writing." Like a fool, I said the first thing that came into my head.

"In that case, we have a fabulous range of ink pens, notebooks, markers and so on." She pointed to the rear of the shop. "Through the arch, there's a little nook."

"Thanks." I didn't need any more stationery or notebooks in my life—I had drawers full—but this gave me an excuse to get away and reconsider what I was even doing here.

"It's a bit cold back there," the young woman told me. "Especially on rainy days. Sorry about that."

"It's fine," I told her. "We can't help the weather." Following her direction to the rear of the shop, I squeezed through the narrow arch. Immediately to my right, stairs led to the upper floor, but directly ahead lay the nook. It had been aptly named. It couldn't have been much larger than my bathroom. Shelves—old ones judging by the colour of the well-polished wood—were laden with baskets of marker pens in every colour imaginable, boxes containing bottles of coloured inks, plastic containers containing erasers, sharpeners, boxes of drawing pins and paper-clips and paper tags. There were staplers and glues, scissors with straight edges, curved edges and serrated edges, and implements that I didn't recognise.

The more expensive ink pens had been locked inside a cabinet with glass doors. I loitered over these. It had been years since I'd used an ink pen. Before me were pens carved from wood, heavily decorated in some cases, or simple and smooth with gold or silver bands or initialling. Oooh, how my little heart coveted one of these beauties!

One day, I promised myself. *When I'm rich.*

I caught the slightest of movements above my head and peered up. There, among brown storage boxes, lurked a magpie. He glared down at me with blue-black eyes, daring me to steal something. I decided he must be the shop's security system. What a great idea.

"Hi," I said.

He nodded his head and thrust out his chest. A. Very. Important. Bird.

With that, I turned my attention to the notebooks. They ranged in size from teeny-tiny—about the size of a postage stamp—to absolutely ginormous. The kind of thing you might see open on a pulpit. They came in every colour of the rainbow—all the tones and shades in between too—and were created from a variety of materials: leather, faux leather, plastic, cloth, hessian, card, paper, cotton ... you name it. I was seriously impressed. Tucked away in the furthest corner was another glass case, though smaller than the one containing all the ink pens. This one housed a small selection of notebooks that were labelled 'grimoires'.

"Fascinating," I muttered. I'd always assumed grimoires were simply plain notebooks containing information gathered by their owners. I frowned into the case. "What's the difference between these and an ordinary notebook?"

"These already contain magick."

I jumped. I hadn't noticed that the shop assistant had followed me into the nook.

"Sorry to startle you," she laughed. "I've had an online order and just need to grab some inks."

"Go for it," I said and stood back as she carefully made her selection, checking the label of each box of ink for a number and comparing it to the printed sheet she held.

"Not a huge difference between some of these greens, but if I make a mistake all hell will break loose," she said.

I smiled and turned back to the grimoires. "What sort of magick do these have?"

"Mostly they keep the contents hidden. Each one comes with a lock spell that you use to hide whatever you've written in there. Woe betide you lose the key!" She laughed merrily. "It's useful for witches and wizards who worry someone else will look inside."

"Indeed," I said, thinking of Murgatroyde's grimoire. "Do you sell many?"

"Some. Not really though. I don't think we're the right store for grimoires. We wouldn't be anyone's first choice. There are a few grimoire shops around, but none in Tumble Town that I'm aware of. You can buy them online, of course."

"Like everything these days," I agreed.

"Speaking of which ..." The young woman showed me her inks. "Better pack these up." She breezed out, leaving me to my own devices once more, albeit under the beady eye of the magpie. I cast another longing look in the direction of the ink pens but instead stepped sideways to study the cheaper notebooks. "I don't need a new notebook!" I reminded myself, but plucked a pretty mauve one from the shelf anyway. A5-sized, with a vegan leather cover and an elasticated closure, I decided it might come in useful for planning a future away from the Ministry of Witches Civil Service. Warming to that idea, I reached for a matching mauve biro and then, despite already having dozens and dozens of pens at home, grabbed a deep purple, a deep pink, two shades of blue, two shades of green, an orange and a red.

Decorative planning. Even if I didn't follow through on any of my hopes and dreams, the colours would look good in my new notebook.

Satisfied, I made my way back into the shop proper and the long counter. The dreadlocked assistant beamed at me. "You've chosen such a pretty notebook," she enthused, beginning to ring through my purchases and drop them carefully into a green-and-white peppermint-striped paper bag. "I hope your cat approves."

Reaching for my purse, I asked, "My cat?"

"The one at the window."

I spun around. The cat, the one that had been hanging around my flat—I mean, it looked identical so I could only surmise that it *was* the same one—perched on the window ledge outside and gazed in at me, its head slightly cocked.

"It's been there since you first came in, so I assumed it was yours."

"Erm ..." I frowned. "Kind of."

"If it's not yours, it's obviously attached itself to you for some reason," the assistant said, holding out the card reader.

"It certainly has." The machine beeped as I flashed my card.

"Thanks so much!" The assistant held the bag for me as I put my card and purse safely away. "See you again sometime!"

"I'm sure you will," I agreed. It was a beautiful shop with lots of gorgeous goodies. I'd be certain to come back. For now, reluctantly, I made my way to the exit ... the rain that streamed from the sky in stair rods ... and the cat.

It watched me with what can only be described as a look of expectation on its sweet, furry face.

Sighing, I stepped outside.

CHAPTER NINE

I sheltered under the shop's canopy for a moment, regarding the cat with a mix of irritation and puzzlement. "What's going on, puss?" I asked. "Why have you followed me?"

It arched its back and stuck its tail in the air, almost as though it wanted me to stroke it. I happily resisted the urge. I hadn't bothered with an antihistamine this morning and didn't fancy sneezing all the way home.

"Yow," said the cat.

"Is that your name?" I asked. "Yow?"

The cat made a noise in its throat I'd never be able to replicate in a month of Sundays, but it was a rolling purr-mix of disdain and despair. Purr-mix? Is that a word? Who cares. It should be.

"Sorry," I said.

The cat jumped from the window, landing lightly at my feet and curling through my legs. As I stared at it, it disappeared from my view and I whirled around to see where it had gone. It turned right and sauntered away, nose in the air, tail high. I watched it go, not remotely interested in following. Back at home there was a couch with my name on it, not to mention that in my bag I had a new notebook and coloured pens! I was going home to dry off, drink tea and play with my new toys.

Nope. I wasn't traipsing after the rotten furball.

Until it turned its head to look at me. "Yow."

We stared at each other. "What do you mean 'yow'?" I asked, my defences beginning to crumble.

"Yow."

It faced forward and resumed its journey. This time, it had a more determined stride.

I took a step after it, then stopped. *No! Couch! Tea! Notebook! Planning!*

"Yow!" the cat called back at me.

"Urgh." *Why the hesitation, Zilla? What are you doing? You should go home!*

Except ...

Hadn't I left home with the express purpose of discovering something about Murgatroyde Plunge and her grimoire? Thus far, I'd failed. All I'd done was spend money. It seemed to me, rightly or wrongly, that there was a connection between the grimoire and the cat. So what choice did I have except to follow it?

Taking a deep breath, I stepped from under the canopy and tentatively followed it down the alley opposite to the way I'd come. The street sign on the side of Pillinger's, high above my head, read *Fire Beacon Lane*—good to know if I became lost. Which seemed likely. I'd never known anywhere more like a rabbit warren than Tumble Town, and Cheapside seemed worse than any other area I'd previously dared venture into.

I was in for a surprise, however. Directly behind Pillinger's I found a burial place. These squares of land, only the size of the footprint of your average house or dwelling, were dotted all around Tumble Town as far as I knew and were repositories for—obviously—the dead. They were multidenominational, in that no matter your creed, colour, religion or paranormal status, you could be buried close to home or have your ashes scattered here among the trees and plants and bushes.

I paused, staring into the fenced-off area. Could this be where Socrates had been found?

"Yow."

The cat appeared to be waiting patiently for me. My head swivelled from it to the burial place and back again. What had Mr Redhill said? He didn't like coincidences. Didn't believe in them. I chewed on my lip, thinking. The cat. The grimoire. The burial place.

"Yow." The cat turned and began to walk away. If I was interpreting this correctly, it didn't want me to stay and explore the burial place; it wanted me to carry on following it.

"Alright," I said, ignoring the thought that I might be placing too much faith in an outlandish notion. "In for a penny, in for a pound."

The further along the lane we ventured, the meaner and smaller the buildings became. Tiddly shop fronts were dotted among the dwellings, with larger windows lit by dingy lighting that illuminated a diverse range of peculiar consumables. A potionery. Vintage books. A haberdashery. A wand shop. Various antique shops or maybe bric-a-brac or junk, it was hard to tell the difference. What amazed me most was that these were evidently doing business—or at least they were *open* for business—whereas the same could not be said for similar shops in the back alleys and lanes around Celestial Street.

Fire Beacon Lane wasn't thronging with folk by any stretch of the imagination, but I did pass people—most of them wearing cloaks or shawls pulled up over their heads—and I had the sense that there were plenty of others around. I just couldn't see them.

I didn't have time to examine the myriad shops that dotted the way—just as well for my bank balance—because the cat kept up a steady pace and I didn't want to lose it. Finally, as the buildings closed in and the lane became almost impossibly narrow, it came to a halt and plonked its furry butt on a doorstep, watching me eagerly as I trailed behind.

"Why are we stopping?" I asked, catching up.

"Yow."

"Yow? Of course, yow. Silly me." None the wiser, I studied the tiny building before me. Evidently once a shop, it stood quiet and sad and slanted slightly sideways as though the house next door was in need of a lie-down and was taking this one with it. Even the front door—a shop door with glass, the wooden surround painted a dull burgundy and absolutely filthy, with rusted brass numbers indicating it was number 113—was lopsided. Beside the door was a big window—also on a tilt—which would once have displayed the shopkeeper's wares but now only provided a frame—rotting and speckled with pigeon droppings—for a filthy pair of net curtains.

"Is this where you live?" I asked the cat.

"Yow." It pawed at the door.

I stood there like an idiot, rain dripping from the hood of my robes and splashing onto my nose, wondering what I should do. "Don't you have a way in?" I asked the cat, but there was no flap in the front door and I had no idea whether there was a back entrance or not.

"Yow."

"I could knock, I suppose," I said, but doubtfully. Imagine knocking on someone's door and asking them to let the cat in and it wasn't even their pet!

"Yow!" The cat tilted its head and widened its eyes.

"Okay, okay ..." Looking left and right down Fire Beacon Lane, making sure I wasn't being watched—at least not overtly—I covered the few paces to the door and knocked smartly.

Rat-a-tat-tat.

Did that seem too official? I grimaced, considering whether to tap again but more softly this time. I decided against it. I can't explain it, but the house just sounded ... *empty*.

"Soz, puss," I said. "I think you're barking up the wrong tree with this one."

"Yow."

"You're right." I corrected myself. "Purring! Purring up the wrong tree." I stepped away from the door. Time to head home. "Anyway, I'm going to leave you here and go home and dry myself off. Good luck."

I began to walk away.

"Yow."

Oh, crikey. Now I felt guilty.

Turning back, I meant to apologise and say good-bye, but as I did so, the door squealed and opened a crack. *Turns out 113 is inhabited after all,* I thought. I hovered in place, the rain pelting down on me, waiting for the door to open wider and the cat to go inside.

Neither of those things happened.

It took me a moment, and then I realised that an eye—attached to a bit of face, obviously—was peeking out at me. I caught my breath, embarrassed and shocked all at once. "Erm ... hi," I said.

"Who is it?" a husky voice asked. A woman's voice, I decided.

"I do beg your pardon," I said. "I'm sorry to have

disturbed you. It's ..." I waggled a wet finger at the cat. "Is this yours?"

The eye disappeared for a moment and I recognised the jangling of a door chain. The woman pulled the door open a touch wider so she could see better. It offered me the opportunity to examine her, too.

She was old. *Really* old. Her pale skin had the look of parchment, dry and papery. Her eyes, a faded blue, were shrunken back into her skull, and her nose, slightly beaked, was threaded with red veins. Her wrinkles were carved so deeply that they might have been a map of hills and valleys—certainly they spoke of a long, eventful life.

Was it me or did she seem somehow familiar?

She brushed her long silver hair over one shoulder and I realised a mouse was sitting beside her ear. "Mine?" she asked, regarding the cat with a keen interest. "I don't believe so."

Oops. "I'm so sorry," I said again. Mr Redhill was right; I *was* forever apologising. "It keeps turning up wherever I am and, erm ... I followed it down here thinking it was coming home."

"I don't recall ever having a cat," the woman said, and the mouse held its tiny paws up to its face and squeaked softly. "Seems to me if he's following *you*, he's decided you belong to him."

It took me a moment to process what the woman had said. For starters, the cat was a he? I'd had no idea. It was good to know. Maybe. However, regardless of its sex or marital status, I had no intention of taking our relationship any further.

"I don't think I belong to him or he to me," I said. "I don't like cats."

The old woman frowned. Her wrinkles changed places. "How can you not like cats? Everyone likes cats."

"Yow," said the cat.

I offered it an apologetic smile. "It's not that I don't like cats, I'm allergic to them," I explained.

"You don't seem allergic to this one," the old woman said.

"I am—" I started to say but stopped. It *had* been a while since I'd sneezed or itched or wheezed or wept in the cat's presence. "Huh. Fancy that."

"Exactly." The woman tottered back and began to close the door.

"I'm so sorry to have disturbed you," I called through the gap. "Thanks for your time."

"Miaoooooow!" The cat suddenly became more

animated. It tipped its head back and yowled. "Rar-rrroooooo. Yooow. Rrrrr!"

The old woman pulled the door open again and listened to the cat for a moment before sighing and lifting her tired gaze in my direction. "It appears you *do* have something that belongs to me, after all."

Puzzled, I shook my head. What could I possibly have that belonged to this old dear?

She raised her eyebrows. "A grimoire?"

My mouth dropped open. You could quite literally have knocked me down with a feather. "You're Murgatroyde Plunge?" I asked in disbelief.

The old woman's gaze skittered up and down the lane. "I'd thank you not to shout about it," she told me glumly. "You'd better come in. I don't want the whole neighbourhood knowing my business."

She opened the door wider and, after a beat, I stepped forward.

"Yow!" said that cat, and I don't think I've ever seen a more self-satisfied smirk on human or beast in my entire life. It lifted its chin and strolled in before me.

Murgatroyde stood back to allow me entrance. "His name is Blue, by the way," she said as I squeezed past her.

"Pardon?" I asked, stepping inside the smoky

interior of the front room. A mean fire burned in a tiny grate, but there wasn't a stick of furniture besides two walls of empty shelving. No wonder the house had sounded so empty when I'd knocked.

"The cat," Murgatroyde informed me. "His name is Blue."

CHAPTER TEN

Murgatroyde directed me through to the rear of the property into a room that resembled both a parlour and kitchen. The fire in here was slightly cheerier and had a trivet over the grate with a warming shelf beside it. Light came from one diminutive window high up on the far wall, a central light hanging over a square kitchen table and several candles burning on floating shelves.

I blinked.

The shelves were *actually* floating in the air, not attached to the wall in any way. Clever. I'd never seen that before.

Blue—if that truly was his name—parked himself in front of the fire and settled into cleaning his paws.

I remained where I was, dripping onto the slate-tiled floor, until Murgatroyde limped in after me.

"Tsk tsk," she said. "Take those robes off and hang them on the door there." She pointed with a gnarly finger to an old wooden latch door on the back wall. I duly did as I was told but kept my bag with me.

"Tea?" Murgatroyde asked, pushing the kettle over the trivet. It swung easily from a bracket with a hook, all rather old-fashioned and quaint but practical too. There were no modern appliances in the room, not even a radio, only the table with two chairs, a small couch and a side table holding a couple of books and some knitting.

"Thanks," I said. "I hope I'm not intruding."

"I rather fear you are," said Murgatroyde, "but not much we can do about it now." She indicated the table. "Do sit down. You're making the place look untidy."

Yes, I could see she might think so. The room, as sparse as it was, was as neat and clean as a new pin. An old wooden broomstick leaned against the wall in the corner, and I found myself wondering whether she swept with it or rode it—and if the latter, did she have a permit? She might be getting on in years and her limbs might be stiff, but she kept an immaculate house.

"All those years inside," she said, as though she could hear my thoughts. "I don't need much. I don't have much. I can do without."

"Do you live in this one room?" I asked, wondering whether she slept on the couch.

She nodded towards the ceiling. "Bedroom's up there. Bathroom out the back."

I'd hate a downstairs bathroom. It would drive me crazy having to come down into the cold every time I needed to visit the facilities in the night.

"Potty," Murgatroyde said, definitely hearing my thoughts.

Wow.

I sat at the table and searched my bag for the grimoire. It had managed to bury itself below everything, but at least it was dry. I drew it out of my bag, wrapped in brown paper, and placed it on the table. If I expected it to suddenly sparkle with new life and reveal all of its secrets, I was disappointed—it didn't bother. In fact, it looked as glum as its rightful owner.

"This came to my apartment block," I told Murgatroyde. "It didn't have a name or address on it. I didn't think it was for me, but it ended up on my doormat. Along with the cat. Blue? Is that what you said he was called?"

"Yes, Blue." Murgatroyde shot a look at the cat. "Stole it, did you?" she asked.

"Yow."

Murgatroyde snorted and began tinkering with an iron teapot, shovelling tea leaves into it. The pot was so flat it looked like someone had stepped on it. The mouse on her shoulder wiggled its whiskers at me, but Murgatroyde remained silent while she located a pair of pottery mugs and a jug for milk.

I felt more than a little guilty as she waited on me. Her knuckles were swollen with arthritis. "May I help at all?" I asked.

"I can manage," she said, somewhat shortly. "I don't have much company, so I like to do everything myself." She reconsidered this and laughed. Or rather hooted. "I don't have any company, come to that. Ever. Just Pip here."

"Your mouse?"

The mouse squeaked. Blue watched with fierce intensity. I wondered if he was hungry.

"Tsk tsk," Murgatroyde said, nudging Blue with her foot. "Nothing for you to take an interest in, little one."

"Yow." Blue settled down comfortably, his eyes

half closed. Murgatroyde might claim not to know the cat, but Blue certainly seemed at home here.

I waited for Murgatroyde to set out the tea things on the table and take a seat opposite me before I indicated the grimoire. "So, this *is* yours?"

She regarded it for a moment, her pale eyes sweeping over the cover. "Perhaps."

What sort of an answer was that? "Perhaps?"

"It could be." She toyed with the teapot but paid no attention to the grimoire.

"But outside ... you knew I had it," I reminded her.

"Blue told me so."

It finally occurred to me that this old woman was crazy. Loop da loop. Chances were Blue wasn't called Blue and hadn't told her anything at all. The woman probably wasn't Murgatroyde Plunge either. That was an assumption I'd made.

Murgatroyde stared across the table at me and I met her eyes.

Yes, they were faded, but her inner light shone brightly with a fierce intelligence. That didn't mean she wasn't completely bonkers, but ... she had mentioned the grimoire without knowing I had one in my bag, *and* she'd mentioned being 'inside'.

She broke eye contact. Pouring tea into one of

the mugs, she pushed it across to me. "Drink," she ordered, and I picked up the mug and gently blew on the steaming liquid to cool it down.

She filled her own mug and held it in her wizened grasp. "I'm tired," she complained. "Ask your questions."

I faltered, unwilling to be drawn into a situation I couldn't handle, but here was an opportunity I'd probably never have again.

"*Are* you Murgatroyde Plunge?" I asked.

She shrugged. "Sometimes I have no idea who I am. I know who I once was."

"Who were you?"

"A teacher," she said without hesitation. "A friend. A lover of life. Of wide-open spaces and fresh air."

"A teacher," I repeated. The newspaper article had said so. Socrates had been her pupil. "Did you murder those children?" The words spilled out of my mouth before I could prevent them. Fortunately—from my point of view—I sounded more curious than accusatory.

"Is that why you're really here?" She sounded weary, and the look that she gave me was daggers.

"No!" I indicated the grimoire. "I followed the cat—"

"Yow," said Blue, and set up to caterwauling. Murgatroyde regarded him with interest before pushing her chin out. "Not my cat."

"But the grimoire—"

"Is of no interest to me. Why don't you keep it?"

"It isn't mine. I wouldn't know how to work with a grimoire."

Murgatroyde, beady eyes raking my face, supped noisily at her tea. She watched me as I took mine and—as delicately as I could—sipped at the liquid. It had an unusual taste. Somewhat sweet. Minty? Or lavender. Bergamot, perhaps. A hint of something ... sweetly oriental. Not unpleasant.

"Blue says you lead a horribly ordinary existence."

I frowned. "The cat said that?"

"Yes. Just now. Didn't you hear him?"

"I heard him yowling—"

"Yow." Blue glared up at me, then gave Murgatroyde a look of pure disgust.

"She doesn't talk cat," Murgatroyde told him.

"Yow!"

Murgatroyde shrugged. "You have to be patient with her."

"Yow."

"Yow? Wow." I huffed down at him. "You come

into my house and make yourself at home and have the cheek to say I have a horrible life!"

"Horribly ordinary," Murgatroyde corrected me.

"There's nothing wrong with being ordinary," I said. "I have a flat, a job ..." *Ugh.* I trailed off. Even I wasn't convinced. "I have a really nice favourite mug—"

Mug? What am I saying?

"Have you never wanted to *be* something else?" Murgatroyde asked. "*Do* something else? Inject a little *adventure* into your life?"

"Yes, but—"

"If you wanted to, you would." Murgatroyde nodded with self-satisfaction. "Many years I spent inside thinking about all the things I could or should have been doing. Now I'm on the outside, but time is short."

I understood what she was implying—grasp the nettle while it's hot, or whatever the saying is—but I wasn't here for a lecture on how to conduct *my* future. I wanted to talk about *her* past. "But the children—"

"The children! The children! Won't anyone think of the children?" Murgatroyde mocked, setting her mug down. "Sometimes it feels that all my life people have been painting me as the witch in Hansel and Gretel." Her tone changed, became raw. "When was the last time anyone took an interest in what *actually* happened?"

As I listened to the pain in her voice, my heart squeezed. "You could tell me," I told her. "I'll listen."

"You'll judge."

"I won't—"

"The whole of society has acted as judge and jury and found me guilty. I'm serving an entire life sentence for something I didn't do."

"I—"

Murgatroyde rubbed her eyes. "You need to leave now. I'm tired."

Oh.

If she'd appeared old before, her skin had taken on a greyish hue now. "I'm so sorry." I carefully slid my chair back. "I honestly didn't come here to dredge up the past. I just followed the cat."

"Blue," said Blue.

I blinked in his direction.

"Yow."

Ha! For a moment there, I thought he'd been speaking to me!

"I'll leave you in peace," I told Murgatroyde, silently wishing her well.

Perhaps she heard my unspoken thought because

she raised her face. "You should take the grimoire," she said.

I shook my head. "I can't. I really have no need of it." I picked up my bag and grabbed my still-damp robes. "I'll let myself out," I said and stepped back into the shop. She followed me. I could feel her eyes burning into my back even as I strolled along Fire Beacon Lane and headed for home.

CHAPTER ELEVEN

Monday came around far too quickly—doesn't it always?—and I arrived at my desk to begin work at 8.20 a.m. Theoretically, I didn't start until half past, but there seemed to be a culture in the office of arriving early and staying late and never moaning about not being paid for the extra hours we worked. I didn't like standing out from the crowd, so in this respect, I followed the herd.

Unpacking my backpack, I chucked my lunch box—cheese and tomato sandwich, bag of plain crisps and an apple—into the desk drawer before carefully pulling out a ratty old pencil case (containing all my new marker pens) and my new mauve notebook. I couldn't resist smoothing the cover but sadly, when I flipped it open, it was as blank as the moment I'd bought it.

Yesterday, Sunday, I'd spent the afternoon sitting on the floor of my living room—alone, because Blue had forsaken me—and tried to find the words in my head that I wished to transcribe onto paper.

MY BIG PLAN? Nope.

BEHOLD THE FUTURE? Nope.

Ambitions? Goals? No, no, no, no, no.

Not even a teeny 'next steps in my life'.

The pages of the new notebook remained pristine.

Why?

Because I was afraid. I was afraid of the unknown. I didn't want to take risks. I didn't want to put myself 'out there', mainly because I had no idea what I'd *find* out there.

Murgatroyde's words haunted me. I'm sure that, had I experienced time in prison, I'd probably want to do more with my life, just as she'd suggested. The thing was, my 'horribly ordinary' life was safe.

And there's a lot to be said for being safe.

"Guys! Guys!" Jess breezed into the office and beamed around at everyone. She'd obviously been in a while, as her coat was draped over her chair and she was carrying a half-drunk cup of coffee.

Ooh. Coffee. That seemed like a top priority. I pushed my wheelie chair back and jumped up, intending to make my way to the kitchenette.

"Cilla!" Jess called, stopping me in my tracks.

Gritting my teeth, I turned back.

"You need to hear this!" she exclaimed, eyes wide. "It's about Lionel."

Lionel?

I peered over. He wasn't at his station. His chair was empty and pushed neatly beneath his tidy desk, his computer screen blank. No bag. No coat. No lunch box. My stomach lurched. How had I failed to notice? Lionel was always in by eight. Every morning without fail. By the time most of us switched our computers on, he'd probably completed half his daily targets.

Ohmygoodness! What if he's— "Is he alright?" I asked, my voice sounding loud and squeaky in the quiet office.

"I should say so!" breezed Jess. "He only went and won the lottery!"

"Which lottery?" Sally asked as my jaw dropped open. "Magick Millions? Daily Dragon?"

"No! The big one! Eurowitches Riches!"

"Eurowitches?" Sally and I repeated in unison.

"Wooo!" Sally collapsed onto her chair in shock.

Unfortunately, as her bottom met the edge of the seat, it pushed it away and she landed heavily on her rump on the floor. Ow.

While Jess and Izo helped her to her feet, I regarded Lionel's empty desk again. *How much did he win?*

Jess must have read my mind. "I don't know the exact amount he won, but I do know that management received an email from him on Saturday night to let them know he wouldn't be returning. He flew to Borneo yesterday."

Cripes! I raised my eyebrows.

"Borneo?" Sally asked.

"Something about the monkeys that he wanted to see."

"Orangutans," I corrected her.

"Whatever." Jess shrugged. "Same thing."

Hardly.

"He's soooooooo lucky!" Sally rubbed her backside.

"Lucky." I nodded, suddenly remembering the coin he'd given me. I patted my pockets. Not there. *What have I done with it? Oh crikey. Please don't tell me I've lost it already!*

Think! I scolded myself. *Where was the last place you had it?*

It came to me. The washing machine. I'd put it on the side. *Fine. It'll still be there when I get home.*

Will it?

It will be if that's where I put it!

"Cilla?" Jess broke into the conversation I was having with myself.

"Hmm?"

"Would you mind clearing Lionel's desk?" she asked.

I opened my mouth, tempted to ask who'd made her the boss all of a sudden, but really? What was the point? Someone had to do it and I didn't mind. It was better than pulling up a permit template and populating it with the details of the next stranger demanding to fly and park their broomstick. "No problem," I told her.

Lionel's personal effects didn't amount to much at all. Firstly, his drawers were practically empty! I mean, what sort of person doesn't have drawers absolutely crammed with all manner of nonsense? Mine were full to bursting. Secondly, most of what I found in them was Ministry of Witches' property. I know this because it said so. All the stationery we used had to be labelled in a particular way, with a logo of a witch's hat surrounded by three small stars. You found the logo on notebooks, on staplers and pencil sharpeners, erasers and even the massive wooden stamps we used to endorse permits. You'd probably find it on paperclips and individual staples if you had access to a particularly powerful microscope!

Besides a ball of elastic bands and a couple of brand-new biros, the only other item of interest was a plastic turtle with a green body, a purple shell and a yellow sunhat, the kind you used to find in children's burger meals. After cleaning the desk and redistributing the stationery to anyone who wanted some (for their own crowded desk drawers), I was left with the pens and the turtle to rehome. By the time I'd fashioned a little flower out of blu tack and stuck it to her hat, it was definitely time for coffee.

I returned to my desk, nursing my mug and gazing alternately at my empty notebook and the turtle. Were there turtles in Borneo? Scrabbling along pristine beaches of golden sand? Had Lionel always dreamed of travelling so far away? Had he thought about orangutans even while stamping his broomstick permits?

The day dragged. Lionel's absence—and the role (or not) that luck had played in that—weighed heavily on my mind. It wasn't that I begrudged him his good fortune ...

Was it?

No. It was something else.

Envy.

I dismissed the word over and over, but it kept popping back. There could be no denying that I was jealous.

Lionel had gained his freedom. He could do whatever he wanted to. Until this weekend, I'd had no desire to change my life. Not really.

But between them, Lionel, Murgatroyde and Blue had messed with my mind. Suddenly I did find myself yearning for something different. For one crazy moment, I half stood and reached for my coat as though I'd leave work midway through my shift and tell upstairs where to stick it!

But that would be career suicide.

And I had rent to pay.

And bills.

And I needed to feed myself.

The phone on my desk rang and I answered it. A long and complicated probate enquiry that required speaking to a number of different departments in the pursuit of pulling up historical data all because someone's nephew wanted a partial reimbursement of an annual broomstick permit that could no longer be utilised by the permit holder because the holder had fallen off her perch and crash-landed in a quarry pit and had therefore been toes up for weeks. Just my luck.

"We can't backdate your claim," I told the woman's nephew, wholly unhelpfully. I hated myself. What a crock of nonsense all this was. Bureaucracy and officialdom. And for what? Pennies!

"May I call you back?" I asked. "The finance team are busy, so there's a delay."

What choice did he have? What choice did I have? Phone plugged to my ear, I picked out the orange marker from my pencil case and occupied myself with a little doodling while listening to Vivaldi's Four Seasons on repeat.

Eventually, 'Lars' in finance—whoever *he* was—offered me the grand sum of thirteen pounds and two lonely pence in remittance for the permit, and I phoned the nephew back to tell him the good news. "The phone call probably cost me that," he complained, and I could only sympathise.

The second I replaced the receiver, the phone rang again. *Am I the only person answering enquiries this afternoon?* I wondered, glowering around at my colleagues. Of course, without Lionel, we were a worker down. Sighing, I reached for the handset, but my eye fell on my doodle.

I'd sketched the outside of a shop. It had a certain familiarity about it. Unknowingly, I'd filled the window with a glorious display—although mainly in orange with a bit of blue and black biro—of books. The phone carried on ringing as I stared down at the image.

In a heartbeat I knew *exactly* what I wanted for my future.

No more permits. No more broomsticks. No Ministry of Witches.

No. I wanted self-employment! My own business! No-one telling me what to do!

A bookshop.

But, pffffft!

How on earth do I manage that?

CHAPTER TWELVE

Stepping out of the Ministry of Witches into the chill evening air felt different.

All around me, my colleagues bustled this way and that—any untucked lanyards flapping in the breeze—hoisting briefcases and handbags into comfortable positions as they dashed for buses or the tube station, for bicycles and e-bikes or, like me, simply began stomping home.

I paused in place, turning about, taking in the blank, tired or sometimes fraught faces. How many of these people were facing redundancy in the latest upheaval? *And it's only Monday*, I thought, making my way over to what would always now be known as Lionel's bench.

I plonked myself down on it—drier this evening

—half expecting Lionel to appear beside me, but of course that wasn't going to happen, given that he was half the world away. Placing my backpack on my knee, I unzipped it and removed the mauve notebook. It was no longer empty. Flipping the soft cover to reveal the front page, I stared at the picture of the —*my!*—bookshop. I'd carefully cut the image from my notepad and then glued it into my notebook. No need for words. This picture spoke volumes.

But—and it was an enormous but—I had a long way to go to achieve my dream.

For starters? Premises.

Celestial Street stretched away from me, affording a wonderful view of the shops and properties lining the road. There were big shops and mini shops and everything in between, but given that retailers were always moaning about rents and rates, how would I ever be able to afford a unit?

Check out rent costs, I wrote on the next page of the mauve notebook. *And rates. Are there any exemptions?* I underlined exemptions a few times and chewed the top of my pen. *Location, location, location!?*

Hmmm.

How much money for stock?

I stared absently at the shop windows nearest

me, full to bursting with colourful wares. *Loads*. I circled the word several times.

Competition? There was a well-established bookshop midway along Celestial Street. It always did great business, not least because it provided one of the few access points from the mundane world. There were a few in Tumble Town that I knew of, and of course, there were some huge online bookstores.

Need to be different, I wrote. *Offer something **SPECIAL**.*

I tipped my head back, staring up at the sky, thinking, thinking … dreaming, dreaming … but then, as my gaze began to fall back down to earth, the back of my neck prickled and I sensed someone might be watching me.

Swivelling my head to the right, I noticed a figure in dark robes, cloaked face angled my way. As soon as I looked directly at them, they turned away.

It might have been nothing at all. Didn't I people-watch all the time?

I decided it was time to make a move anyway. I fancied a hot bath and some more time to reflect on my plans. My insides quivered with what might have been excitement. I couldn't precisely define how I felt because I hadn't experienced it before.

I think perhaps there was a spring in my step as I strolled away from the Ministry of Witches and along Celestial Street, distracted by the window displays I passed, imagining how I could display my own goodies. I spent longer than I needed in front of the Celestial Street bookshop, even snapping half a dozen photos using my phone to record the most interesting book displays.

Finally, belatedly, I arrived at City View Court as night fell. My mailbox contained nothing, not even a circular or a free newspaper, so I wound my way up to the first floor, rummaging in my coat pocket for my keys. Even as I produced them from my pocket, it didn't register that I wouldn't need them. It wasn't until I aimed the correct key at the keyhole that I finally realised the door was already open.

"That can't be," I murmured. "I'm sure I locked it this morning." Why wouldn't I have?

I pushed the door and it swung inwards. "Hello?" I called, as though someone answering me from inside my home would be perfectly acceptable! "Anyone there?"

Please don't let there be.

Holding my breath, I stepped into the hall. One

step. Two. Three. Then I could turn my head to the left and peer into the kitchen.

Stuff on the floor. Broken plates. Broken mugs. *My favourite mug!*

Five more steps. Four. Three. Two. One. Now I could look right into the bathroom. Someone had emptied the bathroom cabinet.

Another few steps and I confronted the truth. The living room had been devastated. My framed pictures and photos had been torn from the walls, plants had been knocked off the windowsill. My books ... what had happened to my books? They'd been torn up! Spines broken, pages ripped out.

Nothing had been left untouched.

I doubled over, unable to breathe, fighting fear and panic. Who had done this? Why?

"Don't touch anything. Don't touch anything," I repeated to myself, over and over, swinging my back-pack to the ground at my feet, searching for my phone. I needed to call the police. My fingers were shaking. Hell! All of me was shaking. I managed to hit the buttons. *Come on!* There it was. The comforting ringing tone. *Come on, pick up!* "Police!" I yelped when they answered, my voice breaking. "I've been— my flat— I've been broken into." I listened.

Half listened. A jumble of words. What were they asking? "Still here?" *Oh, glory, glory, please no!* "No. They're not here." I hadn't checked the bedroom. Suddenly didn't want to see. Such an invasion—

"Yes, please. Yes." They were coming. I hung up. *How long? How long?*

Not sure what to do with myself, I slid over to the window, peering down at the road outside, intending to watch for them. A figure on the pavement on the other side of the road caught my eye.

I shrieked and darted backwards, heart hammering hard against my ribs.

A figure in dark robes. Could it be the one I'd seen outside the Ministry of Witches? Had he followed me home?

Or—

I clamped a hand to my mouth.

Did he already know where I lived? Had he done this?

"Hello?"

A voice called to me from the direction of the front door. "Ms Chaplin? It's the police."

Thank goodness.

"That was quick," I said, rushing back into the hall to meet them. There were two of them. A man and a woman. Uniformed officers.

"We were only down the road," the WPC told me. "Are you alright? You're not hurt?"

"Just shaken," I told her, holding up my hands.

"To be expected," she said. "Do you mind if I take some details?"

I nodded, one eye on the other officer as he poked his head into the kitchen and bathroom and moved past me to scan the living room and bedroom. I shuddered.

Let's all invade my privacy, shall we?

I burst into tears.

A couple of hours later they finally left me alone. Under the officers' patient direction, I'd contacted the landlord to fix the forced door and replace the locks. A forensics team had visited and performed a cursory search for fingerprints or other DNA but, come on. What sort of burglar worth their salt would leave fingerprints in the twenty-first century?

There'd been so many questions and I hadn't been able to answer any of them. No, I didn't have any expensive possessions. No, nothing appeared to be missing. No, I hadn't brought any strange men or women home over the past few weeks. Not unless you included Blue. No, I hadn't been making Witch-toks in the living room.

No and no and no ....

But now ... by myself ... surveying the detritus of my once orderly life, my thumping head threatened to explode. Why would *burglars* destroy my books? What had they been looking for?

"Yow."

I glanced down at my feet. Blue stared up at me. I thought I'd closed and secured the door as best I could. It hadn't prevented this nosy little monster from gaining access though, had it?

"Yow."

"What?" I asked, and even as I did, I realised there *was* one item the burglars may well have been seeking.

Murgatroyde Plunge's grimoire!

And if they'd realised I didn't have it, maybe they'd go looking for her!

"Yow."

"Oh." The realisation was a slap in the face.

"Yow."

"We need to go and find Murgatroyde!" I said, grabbing my coat. "We need to warn her!"

CHAPTER THIRTEEN

"Murgatroyde? Murgatroyde!" Breathlessly, I hammered at her front door. It had been dark for a few hours now, but there were no lights on inside. Maybe I wouldn't see them if she was holed up in the back room. That had seemed to be where she hung out. I twisted the handle but the door was firmly locked. "Murgatroyde!" My fist ached from banging so hard.

"Wha's all the racket?" The voice, a little bit cockney, an awful lot hoarse, seemed to drift out of nowhere. Startled, I twisted to my right. A bald head poked out of next door, all tight skin and huge brown eyes and pointy ears.

"Hi." I recovered myself. "I was looking for Murgatroyde."

"I'd say that was obvious. The 'ole ney-ba-hood knows you is looking for Merg-a-troy, whoever the blazes they might be."

"She," I corrected him. "Your neighbour?"

"I ain't got no neighbour, love. Ain't had a one o' them for donkey's years. Not that side, anyhow."

Stuff and nonsense! "I was only here the other day! You had a neighbour then."

"Imma finking you was imagining it. Or you got the wrong house more 'n likely." The odd creature sniffed in disdain.

I stepped back, checking. "No. This is definitely the right house!" I hammered on the door some more. "Murgatroyde! Murg—"

"If you don't stop that incessant bangin', Imma gonna have to kill ya." The odd little fellow from next door sounded almost regretful about this death threat.

Almost.

I stopped knocking and nervously regarded him. He didn't have a wand. And he didn't *look* dangerous. Even soaking wet, he was probably half my weight. But appearances *can* be deceptive. And this was Tumble Town, after all. I'd been warned many times about the inhabitants of Tumble Town. They had a reputation for being mean and nasty ... and murderous.

I took a step away from him. "I have to talk to her. Have you seen her at all today?"

"Are you finkin' I ain't the full ticket?" the strange fellow asked. "I told ya. There ain't no Merg-ee-toy. There ain't no neighbour. Full stop. The house has been empty a long time. A lonnnnnnnnnnnng time."

"I was only here two days ago!" I protested. "Saturday! I was here on Saturday. I went inside. She was here then!" I stepped forward and walloped the door in frustration.

"Oi!" the little chap bellowed.

I sensed rather than saw faces at other nearby windows, but when I scanned the street, nobody could be seen.

"It's imperative I find her," I said and sniffled.

"Oh, gawd. You ain't gonna cry, are ya? Tell me you ain't gonna cry." He grunted. "Human tears. Ugh."

I rubbed my eyes. Salty tears *were* beginning to squeeze out and spill down my cheeks. "Sorry," I muttered.

"You *are* gonna cry. Eww. So unpleasant."

I snorted hard, trying to gain control of my emotions. "I'm not having a good day," I tried to explain. "Well, I was having a good-ish day. My friend"—not that Lionel had been a friend, not really—"won the lottery and I was happy for him, but then I went home and someone had broken in and my stuff was all over the place and I've had the police around and it's all taken hours. Waaaah!" I couldn't hold myself in check any longer. "Waaaaah!" I wailed.

The neighbour covered his ears. "Stop that caterwauling, will ya?" he squawked. "Waah! See. You've got me doin' it now! Waaaah!"

I glared at him. Was he taking the proverbial? Apparently not. Tears sprung from his eyes like something you might see in a cartoon. I did a double take. But I also stopped my own crying and swiped at my nose, listening to him as he sobbed, his breath hitching, getting stuck in his throat.

"Gosh," I said. "I'm so sorry. I didn't mean to upset you." Maybe I'd touched on a nerve.

He dabbed at his eyes, delicately, as well he might. His nails were long and pointed. I have no idea how he didn't manage to impale his eyeball.

Further down the alley, out of sight around the bend, I heard the sound of a can being kicked. Behind me, someone whispered. *Danger*, I thought they said but, when I jerked around, there was no-one there.

"Who was that?" I asked, eyes darting fearfully in all directions.

"Shadow People," the odd fellow observed, then glanced down Fire Beacon Lane. "In-tress-tin." He pushed his door fully open. "I'm finkin' you'd better come in."

"I don't—" I started to say, but the wind picked that moment to blow hard along the alley, and I heard more whispers.

"Hide. Hide! Danger!"

My legs acted on their own volition, and within seconds I found myself in the odd fellow's old, fusty hallway, and he was quietly closing the door and pushing the bolts home.

I say old and fusty, but perhaps that's not what I mean. Old-fashioned, certainly. The walls were decorated in brown and ochre red. A runner ran the length of the hallway's floor, and it too was patterned with brown and red. A heavy iron radiator—painted cream—took up a fair amount of wall space, and two doors led off the hallway. One of these was ajar.

"Go on through," the little fellow said, and I stepped into his lair.

Of course, it wasn't a lair, it was a parlour. There was a boxy television—so antiquated it had one of those aerials arranged on top of it that look like an alien's antenna—leaving barely enough room for the two-seater sofa and armchair, let alone me and my strange new friend. The television was playing some vintage children's show with a hare, a pig and an ostrich. I had no idea what it might be. He hurriedly switched it off and pulled the curtains tightly closed, then indicated I take the sofa. When I sat, my feet touched his because of how little room there was. He did have extraordinarily large feet, however, encased in a pair of the biggest tartan slippers I'd ever seen.

Aware of how snotty and tearful I was, I fished around in my pocket for a tissue but I was out of luck.

"You want tea?" he asked.

I shook my head, not entirely certain why I'd voluntarily stepped inside this house. *What am I even thinking?* The burglary had me rattled, that's for sure. "No, thank you."

"Somethin' stronger?" There was an air of cunning amusement in his tone. "I don't mind if *I* do," he said and, chuckling, reached inside a cabinet in the nook by the fireplace. The glass doors were tinted brown with etching around the outer edges. I decided that the cabinet must have been there for a hundred years or more. Carefully extracting a bottle, he held it up to the light. It twinkled in ruby and gold. I had no idea what the contents were, but the brand was Aswang.

"I've never heard of that," I said, squinting at the label. "Aswang?"

"Probably best you don't delve too deeply into what aswang are, but I can tell ya, they do make the tastiest spirits."

"Oh." I grimaced, my imagination working overtime.

Perhaps my new friend could tell. "Stick to sprites, piskies and goblins," he said, nodding knowingly, smug in knowledge he didn't intend to share.

"Are you a goblin?" I blurted.

He pouted.

"Not that you look like a goblin," I said uncertainly, hoping he wasn't offended. I don't know many goblins well, but there were a few at the Ministry of Witches. On the whole, witches and goblins are an uneasy alliance at best.

"Not a goblin," he said, settling the bottle on a small side table and reaching for two tiny glasses—

chalice-shaped. "My papa was an Elfman and my mother was a pixie." He caught his breath, then swallowed before beginning to sniffle.

Oh no. I'd made him cry again. "Please don't cry," I begged. "I'm sorry I upset you."

He waved a hand with those long, thin fingers and jagged nails. "I miss them, I does."

"Of course you do," I soothed. "They've passed away, have they?"

"Passed away?" The creature frowned at me. "No. They moved to Costa Rica, they did. My mother likes rainforest."

"Oh."

He snuffled a bit more before unstoppering the bottle—it made a satisfying pop—and pouring a splash of liquid into each glass.

"I'm Zilla," I told him.

"Humphrey," said Humphrey, the Elfman-pixie creature.

Humphrey? Had *anyone* been named Humphrey in the past fifty years? It seemed to me to be one of those names that had all but died out. "Nice to meet you," I told him, glancing at the window. With those thick curtains, it was impossible to see Fire Beacon Lane outside. "I shouldn't be intruding on you."

"Not intruding," Humphrey stoutly replied. "Someone's not nice out there. You should listen to the Shadow People. They always know."

"The Shadow People?" I'd never heard of them. Tumble Town was constantly surprising me. "People who live in the shadows?"

"You never see 'em," Humphrey told me. "But they's always there."

"They said there was danger," I recalled and shivered. Humphrey stared meaningfully at the fire, and it sputtered and blazed a little brighter.

"Someone's following ya." Humphrey handed me one of the tiny glass chalices. I regarded the thick liquid with suspicion. It resembled acrylic paint or nail polish more than alcohol, but it had a sweet, spicy fragrance. The red and gold ebbed and flowed within the bowl, sometimes more red, sometimes more gold. Raising his glass, Humphrey nodded. "Bottoms up!" He tipped his head back, closed his eyes and threw the contents into the back of his mouth. He froze in place for a moment, savouring the flavour, an expression of pure contentment warming his countenance.

Here goes nothing, I thought, and followed suit. The thick liquid hit the back of my tongue and coated my tonsils. It had a velvety texture, and at first all I could taste was a creamy caramel-type flavour—but when the alcohol kicked in, it certainly packed a punch. I managed not to choke—just—but oh boy, did my eyes water.

"Good stuff, eh?" Humphrey asked. "The best. A gift." He forced the stopper back into the bottle and delicately returned it to its place in the glass cabinet. "Expensive, so it is."

"Delicious," I said, because now that the fire in my throat had gone out, all I could taste was cream caramel, and I rather liked that. Whatever the liquid was, it had warmed me through and helped me feel a little steadier, emotionally at least. "Do you think it's safe for me to go outside yet?"

What would the Shadow People say?

Humphrey shrugged. "I wouldn't."

It struck me that this wasn't particularly helpful. "But—"

"Look, see, if you's going to be a-knocking and a-hollering on next door, you's just going to be drawing attention to yerself. Seems to me like someone is following ya, so if I was you, which I ain't, thank goodness, I'd hang out 'ere a while."

I slumped on the sofa.

"What've you got that someone else wants?" Humphrey enquired, then wafted one of his spidery hands at me. "Nah. Scrub that. Don't tell me. Least said and all that."

"I haven't got anything!" I protested. "Honestly! I came home from work and found someone had broken into my flat." I held up my hands. "I'm not carrying anything! Hell, I didn't even bother locking my front door—mainly because the lock is broken—but there was no point anyway. The flat is ransacked. Nothing has been taken. All I have is my phone and my purse. That's it!"

"Oh dearie, dearie me!" Tears rolled down Humphrey's pale cheeks. "That's a terrible story, that is."

"Please don't upset yourself," I begged, my own eyes filling up yet again. Honestly! Where do all our tears come from?

"I'm truly sad for ya," said Humphrey, crying harder. "'Specially cos they's probably after yer personage rather than yer belongings."

"My what? My personage?"

"Yerself. They's probably coming after *you*!"

I stared at him in absolute horror. It hadn't occurred to me that I might be in danger. "But I'm nothing!" I told him. "I issue permits. Broomstick permits. I live a dull, ordinary"—I was beginning to hate that word—"life. I assumed—rightly or wrongly

—that it was Murgatroyde's grimoire that they were after ..."

We regarded each other for a long moment, the only sound the crackle of the fire.

"Were you telling the truth when you told me Murgatroyde didn't live next door?" I asked, my voice soft, my eyes beseeching.

Humphrey gave me a hard stare, his lips pressed tightly together. Finally he sighed and jerked his head towards the door. "You'd better come see," he said.

CHAPTER FOURTEEN

I'd wondered what was around the back of these little dwellings when I'd walked along Fire Beacon Lane before. Well, now I found out.

Humphrey led me through his teeny kitchen, with some interesting 1980s tiling and shelves full of curios and vintage oddities, and through the reinforced back door into a tiny yard. He kept pots and planters full of flowers and small, curated bushes. Maybe those impossibly long fingers of his were green after all because, despite not having access to much daylight in the narrow confines between buildings, his mini garden was flourishing.

Stepping out of his back gate into a narrow ginnel, we turned left. Murgatroyde's house didn't have a yard as such; the back door opened directly onto the alley. Unlike Humphrey's door, this one wasn't reinforced. It was old and scuffed, the wooden planks worn at the edges, the paintwork ragged and peeling.

I stood in front of it, waiting for Humphrey to produce a key.

"'Tis open," he said. "You can go straight in."

Bemused, I twisted the round handle and the door swung inwards. Inside, the building was dark, so I fumbled around until I located a light switch. It took a moment for the electricity to reach the bulb, but eventually the light blinked on and slowly began to warm up.

Had it only been a couple of days since I'd been sitting in this kitchen with Murgatroyde? How could that be?

Then, it had been scrupulously clean and tidy. There had been the small sofa, the table, the chairs. There had been a rug, mugs, a kettle, a teapot. There'd been a fire burning and shelves with her belongings. Okay, there hadn't been much, but it had resembled a home of sorts.

Now? Well ...

Unlike my flat, this home hadn't been turned over. It hadn't been burgled. It hadn't been the victim of bored or loutish teenagers. Graffiti hadn't been daubed all over the walls, and there was no drug paraphernalia—or worse—underfoot. It simply looked like a kitchen that hadn't been used in decades. The broomstick in the corner—it must have been the same one I'd seen before—was covered in lacy cobwebs. Strings of dusty webs hung from the ceiling, catching at my face. *Ugh*! The floor was filthy, the range covered in a lifetime's worth of dust. The areas around the light switches and the door handles were grimy with sticky fingerprints. As I stood there, staring around the room in disbelief, a cockroach scuttled out from beneath the broomstick, paused a moment to regard the intruder—me—and dived between the floorboards.

I jerked away from it, my heart beating. "This is impossible," I said. "I was only here two days ago. It can't look like this—"

Retreating, I pulled open the door in the corner where my damp robes had hung. Inside was a compact bathroom with a sink, a bath and a loo. This was why Murgatroyde had less of a yard than Humphrey. Her bathroom had been added on after the house had been built.

"And yet the truth is before your eyes," Humphrey said. He'd hung back, but now he stepped into the kitchen after me.

Turning to him, I gestured at the space where the table had been. "I sat here having tea with Murgatroyde Plunge—"

"Must've been another house. Another woman. Pullin' yer leg."

"No!"

"Murgatroyde's dead at least ten year," Humphrey told me. "Maybe twenty. Maybe more. I forget. Died, she did."

I shook my head. This was crazy. Maybe *I* was crazy. I wanted to weep again, but I was frightened I'd set Humphrey off. At the same time, I must confess this was scaring me. After everything that had happened over the past few days, I was beginning to feel like my life was out of my direct control. It felt as though someone else was pulling my strings, and I could only react to what was happening.

"No," I repeated. "I'm not having it!"

Stomping across the kitchen, I pulled open the door to the front room, the shop. This looked much as it had the other day. Dusty and dank and empty. Heavy nets obscured my view of Fire Beacon Lane but allowed a little orange light to filter through. For a moment I thought I saw a shadow bobbing around before the window. Imagining someone out there, perhaps waiting for me, my skin tingled, alert to danger. It quite took the wind out of my sails. Nonetheless, I marched to the internal door opposite the front door and yanked it open, expecting Humphrey, who'd reluctantly followed me, to protest. He remained silent so I squeezed through and groped about, searching for another switch that would illuminate the dark stairs. I found one, but unfortunately nothing happened. I peered up at the dark hole at the top of the stairs. What was up there? What was waiting for me?

Swallowing my fear, I climbed the first step. Then the second. I stumbled on the third and belatedly remembered I had my mobile phone on me. I fished it out and switched on the torch. *Why didn't I think of this sooner? I'm not firing on all cylinders ...*

The oak stairs—neither painted nor carpeted—crept crookedly up and away from me, each step a different height and depth than the last. Without a torch, I'd probably have fallen up them and broken my neck. Coming down I'd have broken it twice.

I navigated the whole creaking flight with some difficulty and made it to the landing. There was no bulb in the light fixture, which explained why the switch downstairs hadn't worked. On the narrow landing I found myself faced with two final doors, both standing ajar. The front room was empty, the old-fashioned wallpaper ditsy but faded. Cautiously stepping inside, I surveyed the space. Calm, quiet, empty. Within seven or eight steps I was at one of the two windows that overlooked the alley. Leaning forward, I peeped out. There *was* someone out there, hanging around in the doorway opposite. Dark robes. I couldn't see much more.

Waiting for me?

Hmm.

Backing up, I retreated onto the landing and turned to examine the back bedroom. This one, over the kitchen, contained an old iron bedstead with a stained, saggy mattress. Built-in cupboards filled the alcoves on either side of the fireplace. The walls had been lined with striped paper, olive and cream with hints of red threaded through. It might have looked cosy and homely once, but now it spoke of people long gone. This room hadn't been slept in for years.

I took one step forward. Glass crunched below my boot. Squatting down, I noted an object leaning against the wall. A photo frame, maybe twelve by ten inches, the outer edge laced with silver. I didn't expect to find a photo inside, but I was wrong. A faded image of a wizard with an impressive beard and moustache, looking directly at the photographer while holding an open book in both hands, gazed out at me.

Who are you? I wondered.

From the bottom of the stairs, Humphrey hissed at me. "Everythin' alright up there or wot?"

"Yes," I called back softly, tucking the broken photo frame carefully under my arm and scanning the rest of the room. Nothing else of interest. I wandered over to the small window here. It afforded a view over neighbouring rooftops out the back but not a lot else.

As I turned back for the door, a sudden, quick movement caught my eye. A mouse! I watched as it loped for the cupboard to the right of the fireplace and disappeared through the tiniest gap. I might have been repulsed—*ewww! Rodents!*—but hadn't Murgatroyde had a mouse? Okay, this probably wasn't the same one, but it was the only link I had to her existence.

Besides, I should have been checking out the cupboards anyway.

After long years of damp and disuse, the cupboard door had bowed and stuck to the frame, but a hard tug and it came free, exposing half a dozen empty shelves.

Or at least I thought they were empty until I

waved my mobile around. There, right at the bottom, tucked in the corner and wrapped in brown paper and string, was a book-sized parcel. Holding my breath, I reached for it, only to jerk my hand away when I realised the mouse was standing like some kind of sentinel beside the package, washing its whiskers while keeping a beady black eye on me.

Do mice bite? I asked myself, knowing the answer was 'probably'.

"You don't want to bite me," I whispered, tentatively stretching out my fingers. "Do you?"

The mouse stopped fiddling with its whiskers and squeaked at me. We stared at each other for an impressively long time before the mouse finally backed off. Relieved, I slid the parcel out from its dark, dusty corner.

"Thank you," I said. Politeness matters.

Clutching the parcel and the photo, I side-stepped to the cupboard on the opposite side of the fireplace. This one turned out to be a wardrobe, with hanging space for all your robes. I tapped on the back, seeking hidden passages, but the wall was solid. Unable to find Narnia, I headed back down the stairs, sliding my free hand against the wall and taking great care, finally joining Humphrey at the bottom.

He pressed a finger to his lips and pointed at the door. I froze, cocking my head to listen. Something metallic scratched at the door. Probably the lock. Did someone have a key? Or were they trying to break in?

I leaned over and whispered in Humphrey's enormous pointy ear. "Time to make ourselves scarce."

He nodded, eyes watering, and slid silently towards the door into the parlour. I followed him, doing my best to glide to draw as little attention to myself as possible. Once inside the kitchen, I closed the door firmly. There was no lock on this one, and I looked around for something to jam the door in place. My eye fell on the broomstick. I tugged it free of its cobwebs, disturbing several of the most enormous spiders I had ever seen, and wedged it underneath the handle. Humphrey was already outside, so I joined him, flicked the light switch off—thereby plunging Murgatroyde's house into darkness—and rammed the door closed.

It was probably my imagination, but I could almost feel someone's breath on my neck.

I bolted after Humphrey.

CHAPTER FIFTEEN

Within moments we'd scuttled inside Humphrey's house and secured his back door. We stood facing each other, both of us pale and wide-eyed—well, Humphrey was pale and wide-eyed, and I assume I was too because that's how I *felt*—and listened for movement.

Humphrey chewed on a knuckle, his eyes swimming.

"Don't worry. They won't follow us." I had no idea whether they would or not. I supposed it would depend on whether they knew where we'd disappeared to. "Let's go back into the front room," I whispered.

He nodded and led the way, switching off all the

lights as we went, until we were alone in the front room with only a single lamp burning in the corner.

"I have to admit I'm spooked," I told him, keeping my voice low, as though whoever had been trying to break into next door would be able to hear us.

"Humphrey too," said Humphrey, clutching his chest and glancing towards the curtained window.

Blimey. Don't die on me, I telegraphed. "I have no idea what's going on, but I need you to tell me all you know about Murgatroyde Plunge," I told him.

"What 'ave ya there?" Humphrey asked, grimacing at the objects I held in my hands.

Setting my mobile aside, I narrowed my eyes. "You spill your secrets and I'll spill mine."

"Meh." He didn't like that, but I could see he was dying to look at the parcel. "I ain't lyin'," he said. "Well, maybe a few misrepresentations of the truth, but nuffin' serious. Murgatroyde died a long time ago."

This couldn't be true, but I didn't interrupt.

"She lived next door for many years. This used to be my grandparents' house, and then my old folks lived 'ere too ... till they took it on themselves to seek out warmer climes." He sniffed. "Abandonin' me in the process. Anyway, Murgatroyde taught at Hecate

Primary long before Humphrey came along. May have taught my papa. Then she did a bad thing and whoosh!" He mimed an explosion with his long fingers. "Prison. Long time. Died." He sat back on his armchair and regarded me expectantly. "Your turn."

"Not so fast," I said, making sure the parcel was comfortable on my knee. "Tell me how it is that I spent some time with her *in her house*"—I pointed at the wall—"just two days ago?"

To his credit, Humphrey did give this some thought. "Obviously, that's not possible unless Murgatroyde is a ghost or somefink, and someone did magick."

This stopped my thought process in its tracks. "She seemed pretty solid to me," I said, but then her parlour had been clean and warm and inviting, as had her tea. "Why is her house still empty? Did anyone inherit it?"

Humphrey shrugged. "No family to sort it out. She lived alone."

"There must have been some relative," I said, "no matter how distant."

Humphrey pulled a face, clueless. "Not that she told me about."

Wait a minute! "You met her?"

Humphrey jerked back in shock.

"So, what aren't you telling me?" I asked.

He hesitated, his enormous eyes looking everywhere except at me. Eventually he gritted his teeth and peeped over at me. "Murgatroyde came out of prison. She moved back into her house. She tried to live her life again. But she died within a few months." He began to cry. "I liked her. She didn't seem like a wrong'n to me. She told me she was innocent and I believed her, I did!"

"Wow," I said. "And how long ago was this?" I expected Humphrey to say 'recently', but he only cried harder.

"Years ago," he said. "Years and years."

None of this made any sense to me, but at least Humphrey had come clean. I patted his knee.

He nodded, scooped a huge handkerchief out of his pocket and blew his nose hard. "Humphrey's okay," he said. "Your turn." He pointed at the parcel.

I pulled at the string, struggling to undo the knot. Humphrey leaned forward and, before I could protest, sliced through the string with a nail. I allowed the paper to slip away from the contents and wasn't remotely surprised to find the grimoire inside.

"What's that?" Humphrey sounded disappointed.

"It's Murgatroyde's grimoire." I sighed. "I tried to

give it back to her, and here it is turning up like a bad penny!"

"How'd ya give the book back? You wasn't alive when Murgatroyde lived 'ere. Did you see her in prison? You was only a kid."

"Have you listened to a word I said?" I hissed. "I saw her two days ago!"

"Meh."

"Meh," I responded likewise, flipping the cover to view the beautifully illustrated meadow and the dandelion seeds floating across the page. I flipped over the next few pages, warmed by the illustrations. Was it my imagination, or did the journal feel thicker again? The pages too. And not because they were damp, but because there were more of them of a better quality than before.

Perhaps this wasn't the same grimoire after all?

But it had to be. There was no escaping that front page. You couldn't create that twice.

I showed it to Humphrey. He caught his breath and his eyes became watery. He reached out to thread his fingers through the grass. I let him do so; at the end of the day, the grimoire did not belong to me. While he flipped through the pages, I tipped the photo frame upright and stared at the wizard in the image.

"Do you have any idea who this is?" I asked.

Humphrey cast a cursory glance. "Nah."

"Was Murgatroyde ever married?"

Humphrey shook his head.

"Is the person in the photo old enough to have been her father? I mean, the photo isn't ancient. It's colour for starters and has that kind of seventies tint to it. How old would her father have been in the seventies? What do you think?"

Humphrey gazed blankly at me.

"Could be sixties, I suppose." I could see I was on my own with this. "I'm wondering why the only things that remained next door were the photo and the grimoire. There must be a connection that—"

I broke off. Humphrey had come to the end of the entries in the grimoire. Or at least the entries that had disclosed themselves thus far. Beneath his spidery hands, pencil marks were beginning to reveal themselves—scratches and whorls now as familiar to me as my own handwriting.

"Let me see that," I said and slid the book from Humphrey's grasp. He leaned closer as I turned the grimoire this way and that, trying to catch the marks in the right light.

"There's a sketch," said Humphrey.

There was, in varying shades of grey, the beginnings of an outline, but its grand reveal had stalled. I tried to warm the page using my palm, but nothing happened. Grunting, I pushed the book back towards Humphrey. "Lay your hands on it," I said, wondering why it was working for him but not for me. "Maybe whatever this is relates to you."

Twittering nervously, Humphrey placed both hands on the pages. A few seconds later he raised them again. I thought he'd removed them too prematurely, but actually, the image had taken shape and now I could clearly see the same wizard from the photo.

"Do it again," I ordered, "but for longer."

Humphrey, brow furrowed, lay his palms down. This time he remained still for what seemed like hours but was probably only about thirty seconds. "Lift! Lift!" I said, unable to bear the anticipation much longer. Humphrey did as he was told, and I spun the grimoire to get a better look. The only difference between the photo and the sketch of the wizard—now taking on some pale colour as though parts of it had been filled in with watercolour—was that the book he held in his hand was heftier, and a meadow was springing forth from it.

This was a drawing of a wizard holding Murgatroyde's grimoire.

"What does that say?" Humphrey asked.

I hadn't noticed the writing, so pale were the pencil marks, but as I squinted at the page I could begin to make out some of the words.

"Dodo," I read. "Does that say ice? No. It's an I ... no ... not an I, a one. One ... two ... five ... zero? 1250 Bodor, no, Tudor! Tudor! 1250 Tudor Lane." I gazed at Humphrey expectantly. "Where is Tudor Lane?"

Humphrey stared at me with huge eyes. "Back towards Celestial Street and turn right."

"You'll have to show me!"

"Not I," said Humphrey, pointing at his wrist. I have no idea why he did that, because he wasn't wearing a watch, but I understood his meaning. My mobile phone's screen told me it was 21.42.

"Do you think it's too late?"

"Too late for Murgatroyde," said Humphrey, matter of factly. "She's dead. And too late for Humphrey. I'm a-needin' my beauty sleep."

"Will you come with me tomorrow?" I asked, belatedly remembering I was supposed to be at work as normal in the morning.

"Absolutely not," said Humphrey.

A loud thud, ridiculously close, followed by a crash, shocked us both into silence. A moment later, glass shattered. What on earth was happening?

I grimaced. "Next door?" I whispered.

Humphrey nodded.

"What are they after?" Both of us eyed the grimoire. "Should we call the police?" I asked.

A look of perfect astonishment washed over Humphrey's face. "You don't live in Tumble Town, do ya?"

"Erm ..."

"No-one calls the fuzzies hereabouts."

"Oh." I swallowed. "But I need to get home."

Humphrey winced, wrinkled his nose and shook his head. "Not now. Not a good idea."

I puffed my cheeks out. I didn't much fancy edging past next door, not if they were looking for the grimoire. "Do you mind if I wait here awhile?"

Humphrey pointed at the sofa. "I'll fetch a blanket."

CHAPTER SIXTEEN

I didn't make it to work the next day.

I don't know why I imagined I would.

I'd eventually—once the banging and crashing had stopped next door—fallen into an uneasy doze on Humphrey's miniature sofa with my knees up around my neck. At some point I must have relaxed enough to fall more deeply into sleep because when I opened my eyes it was daylight and Humphrey, wearing a cheap but smart suit, was holding a mug of pungent coffee under my nose.

I blinked and pushed myself upright, my shoulders and knees going off like firecrackers. *Ow!* "Morning," I said. "Sorry, I thought I'd have been gone by now." I hurriedly checked the grimoire was where I'd left it last night, tucked down the side of the sofa, within reach of my fingers.

"Probably best you stayed," Humphrey replied, his voice gruff.

"It's incredibly kind of you to take a stranger in," I said, taking the mug of coffee from him.

He shrugged and blushed. A bit of a sweetheart under that grouchy exterior, I decided.

"Thanks for the coffee." I indicated his suit. "What time is it? Do you need to get to work? I can go." I cocked my head, listening for sounds from next door but couldn't hear anything.

"No rush," said Humphrey, but I didn't entirely believe him.

"Where do you work?" I sipped hurriedly at the coffee. Brother, it was strong!

"Wiztec Distribution," said Humphrey. "Heard of it?"

"No," I admitted.

"It's a warehouse," Humphrey said. "I work in the office."

"Nice. What do you make?"

"We don't make nothing," Humphrey told me. "We *distribute*."

Oh yeah, like that's what distribution means. "Got ya. What do you distribute?"

"Wizard technology," Humphrey told me.

This conversation was going nowhere fast. I swallowed more coffee. "Right."

After a pause, Humphrey finally added, "Wands and orbs and robes and spellbooks and staffs and that manner of junk. Made in China. Shipped here for global distribution. The irony is we then ship back to Japan, Thailand and the rest of Asia."

"I see," I said.

"But it's a job ..."

"I rubber-stamp permits for broomsticks," I said.

Humphrey shuddered. "Good grief. I thought my job was boring."

For some reason I found this funny and choked on my coffee. While I swabbed madly at the front of my robes, my phone began to ring. It was my landlord. After a quick conversation, I hung up and threw back my blanket. "I have to go. There's a locksmith coming out to fix my front door."

Humphrey nodded.

"I don't suppose I could quickly borrow your facilities, could I?" I asked.

Humphrey pointed me upstairs. "First door on the right. Don't eat the toothpaste."

Why would I eat the toothpaste?

The layout of Humphrey's home was similar to

Murgatroyde's but with a front room instead of the shop, and upstairs, the back room had been carved into two to house a diminutive but beautifully clean bathroom and what I assumed was either a cupboard or a box room. The door was closed so I couldn't tell.

Rejoining Humphrey downstairs, I found he had donned a plain grey robe and was carrying his lunch bag. I wondered if his lunch bag contained the same boring rubbish mine did.

"Ready?" he asked and unlocked the front door.

Collecting the grimoire, the broken photo frame, my phone and purse, I went out first and turned to watch him lock up. "Thanks again."

"Yer welcome."

"Have a good day at work."

"You too." He pocketed his keys.

I smiled, feeling awkward and turned away, beginning to walk along Fire Beacon Lane past Murgatroyde's.

Footsteps followed me and I turned back. "I go this way too," said Humphrey.

"Oh." Now I felt like a total fool.

Humphrey indicated Murgatroyde's. "Bit of a mess."

The shop window had been broken and the front door forced. It reminded me of home, and I realised with a sinking feeling that I had to go back there and face that violation once more. My eyes welled up.

"It's horrible," I sniffed.

"I'll make a call," Humphrey said, sounding choked too. "Get some boards put up."

I wondered who he'd call or who would foot the bill. "That's properly community-spirited," I said. "I can't imagine anyone doing that for me."

He snuffled. "It's important to do what we can."

We walked on in silence until we reached the art and craft shop, where the route diverged into four new paths. "I go that way," I said, pointing diagonally—ahead and to the right.

He nodded and indicated the path left towards the river.

"Take care." I began to walk away but didn't make it more than six steps before I turned about. "Humphrey?" I called after him.

He too stopped and turned around.

"Are you sure you don't want to come with me to find this Dodo person? We could go this evening."

"Absolutely not," said Humphrey.

I sighed, disappointed. I don't know why. I think I just wanted to prolong my encounter with him. "Alright," I said. I'd tried. "Bye."

"Bye."

I spent the morning tidying and cleaning while waiting for the locksmith to arrive. It was depressing how little of what I owned was worth saving. My books were in tatters. Not a single one of them had survived. The cushions on my sofa had been sliced open and the stuffing removed. Rugs had been pulled up and cut up. Even my bedding and mattress had been shredded. I spent most of the morning stuffing my life into bin bags and crying pitifully until belatedly realising, just short of midday, that I hadn't phoned work.

Oops.

"Hi, Izo," I said when he answered his phone. "Ah, I apologise for the late notice, but I'm not going to be in work today."

"I'd figured that out," Izo said.

"I'm sorry," I repeated. Always sorry. "Someone broke into my flat while I was at work yesterday. Everything's a mess—"

"Oh dear." He didn't sound like he cared particularly. But why should he? It hadn't happened to him. I tried not to let my irritation bubble over.

"I'm waiting for a locksmith," I explained.

"Will you be in tomorrow?"

I opened my mouth to say yes, of course I would be, but stopped myself. The past few days had been traumatising and gut-wrenching, and keeping Izo happy had suddenly become the least of my worries. "No," I told him, genuinely astonished to hear the word form out loud. "I need a few days to sort everything out." Myself included.

"Ah, okay." Izo sounded surprised too. "No problem. I'll let HR know."

I bet you will, I thought. *And they most certainly won't hold me to account when it comes to handing out jobs in the shake-up, will they?*

"Rightio," I said, hanging up on him before I could say anything I'd regret and reaching for yet another black bin bag.

By the time the locksmith made an appearance, I'd moved on from my bedroom and the living room and into the kitchen. The fact was I was hungry and thirsty and needed to sort this space out so I could at least have a cup of tea!

"Would you like a tea or coffee?" I asked the young man fiddling with my lock, hoping he'd say no.

I wasn't entirely sure I had two usable mugs left. At least the kettle was still in one piece.

"Coffee would be awesome," he said. "Milk and three, cheers love."

Love? He's younger than me!

And *three* sugars? Excessive. I considered charging him. Maybe I should open Zilla's caff. But no, I wasn't sure I could stand the smell of frying all day.

A quick shufty through my cupboards confirmed that most of my crockery had been broken, including, you'll remember, my favourite mug. Tears sprang into my eyes once more as I crouched on the floor, collected the pieces and considered gluing it back together. But what would the point be? In the end, I shovelled it up along with everything else and double-bagged all of the kitchen debris. I didn't want the refuse collectors cutting themselves. However, I did find a couple of old camping mugs—I mean, *camping*? I hadn't been camping since I'd been a girl guide *years* ago!—in the back of the cupboard, so the locksmith and I managed to sate our thirst at the same time and I didn't have to resort to drinking out of a saucepan.

While the locksmith finished up, adding a couple of new bolts to the top and bottom of the door, I rescued the dustpan and brush and swept in all the corners where my big brush couldn't reach. This was a chore I hadn't attacked for a while, and I found a couple of elastic bands, a plastic token for a supermarket trolley, a girl's hair slide—definitely not mine—numerous dried-out peas, one rotten cherry tomato and more dust, fluff and hair than reasonably had a right to be anywhere near a kitchen. Most importantly, when I pulled out the washing machine to access the very darkest corners, I spotted the token.

Lionel's coin.

I fumbled for it, but it had stuck to the floor. Eventually I managed to slide it out, easing my thumbnail beneath it to pick it up. Sitting back on my haunches, I turned it over and over. No longer shiny, it was covered in a greasy layer of old washing detergent.

"Cheers, love." The locksmith, holding his tin mug out, peered into the kitchen. "All done."

I stood—with difficulty because I was so stiff from a night on Humphrey's sofa—and took the mug from him. "Thanks."

He handed me my new keys. "All yours. If you have any problems, let your landlord know and I'll come and sort things out."

The coin burned in my hand. Setting down the

locksmith's empty mug and the new keys, I regarded the coin, remembering what Lionel had told me. I could do with some luck. Without thinking, I held the token out to the locksmith.

"A friend of mine gave me this," I told him. "He said one day I would meet someone who would need some good luck."

"Oh yeah?" The locksmith regarded the grubby coin with more than a touch of derision.

"He said if I willingly gifted it to such a person, good luck would come to us both."

"Is that right?"

"Yes. The only thing is, one day you have to give it to someone else in the same way."

"Aha."

"Would you like it?" I asked, considering whether to flip it as Lionel had done. Knowing my luck, neither of us would catch it and it would roll between the floorboards.

"Yeah, why not," he said and took it from me.

CHAPTER SEVENTEEN

"Grrr."

Standing beneath a handy—albeit almost useless—street light, I twisted my phone sideways. Of course, the image I was studying turned sideways too. "Argh."

Grunting, I carefully removed the grimoire from my bag. This evening I'd chosen to wear a cross-body, heavily embroidered cotton bag someone had brought me back from India. It wasn't waterproof, but at least I could keep it close to me. Right on my hip, in fact. I'd decided that a backpack could be too easily accessed and, at the moment, the grimoire was probably my most precious possession.

Given the state of my flat, what else did I have left?

"One two five oh," I said, muttering to myself. "It definitely says that."

"Does it?" a voice whispered, so close to my ear they could have licked the lobe. I jerked my head sideways. No-one there. Not really. These 'Shadow People' took a bit of getting used to.

The problem was that the addresses on Tudor Lane only went up to three hundred and fifty-seven. How did I know? Because I'd walked the whole length of it. At the very bottom of the lane, where the houses became smaller, older and in worse condition, you had to take a right onto River Way. I'd decided against that because I'd heard that Deadman's Wharf—if that's where River Way led—right on the Thames was as rough as sandpaper.

And I didn't need any more drama in my life.

"There is no one two five oh," I reiterated, resisting the urge to howl in frustration.

"No one two five oh," mocked the whisper.

"Never 'as been!" another voice cackled.

"Oo you calling an 'as-been?"

I rolled my eyes. How charming these Shadow People were, in a super-annoying-don't-strangle-them-all-at-once way. "You could be more help," I muttered.

"You could get yerself to the hop-tish-huns," said the first whisper.

I wondered if there was any way to turn these beings off or shoo them away. Anything. I was beginning to question my sanity. "It says one two five oh!" I protested, but, squinting at the pencil markings once more, I had a fancy that the oh wasn't an oh at all. "Oh." I chewed my lip. "Is it a *c*?"

A *c*?

125C Tudor Lane? Would that make sense?

I retraced my steps. The odd numbers were on one side of the alley and the even-numbered addresses faced them. The alley itself was wider in some places than others, six feet at its narrowest, maybe fourteen or fifteen at its widest—mainly where the larger houses faced warehouses. The houses and factories were interspersed with individual shops. A convenience store—of sorts—next door to a tobacconist. Further down the lane was a rope shop. Yes, a shop dedicated to selling rope and string.

Bizarre.

On my way up I'd passed a baker's, a greengrocer's and a pub, curiously named The Pig and Pepper. And a hat shop.

And here it was again. The Hat and Dashery.

Coincidentally, this was 125 Tudor Lane. I studied the sign.

125 Tudor Lane. Proprietor Hattie Dashery.

So, would 125C be two doors down? I stepped back for a better view. No. It definitely wasn't. 127 and 129 were three-storey houses, pretty much like Hattie Dashery's but without a shop front. However, to the left of the mahoosive glass window housing an extraordinary display of the most incredible top hats I had ever seen was another door.

A blue cat sat on the step there and purred up at me.

"Blue?"

"Yow."

"You get around," I said, joining him on the threshold, all the better to read the brass plaques to the right of the door.

"Yow."

"125B Hattie Dashery. 125C Wonderland Detective Agency?" I backed away from the door and studied the upper floors. "A detective agency? Why would the grimoire send me here?"

"Yow." Blue pressed his nose against the door.

"Okay, okay." Pulling my bag close, I pushed it open. I couldn't see anything telling me to keep out. I glanced back at Blue. He hadn't followed me in.

"Yow!" He stuck his nose and tail in the air and marched away.

"Bizarre little thing," I whispered and turned my attention to the steep flight of stairs ahead of me. They were inviting me to climb, so I did so. By the time I'd reached the first landing, I was holding onto the balustrade. The long landing had just the one door, evidently where Hattie the milliner resided. I paused outside this and caught my breath. Then it was on to the second flight of stairs—and this one seemed even steeper. At least the lights were on and I could see where I was going. I climbed onto the second landing, hauling on the newel post to drag my unfit backside up. Panting, I allowed myself a moment to recover before tapping on the door. Another brass plaque here. This one read:

Wonderland Detective Agency.

Licensed to Investigate. MOW ZXGHT076577612.

Proprietor: Elise Liddell.

Before I could tap on the door, a tall young man with dark, spiky hair pulled it open and did a double take. "Whoa!" he said, rearing away from me. "I didn't realise anyone was out here!"

"Sorry!" I puffed and laughed. "I thought the whole neighbourhood would be able to hear me panting!"

He laughed, adjusting a woollen scarf around his shoulders. I wondered why he was wearing it. The evening was cool but not freezing. He did look rather suave though. "The steps normally creak horribly," he said. "That's the early warning system we're used to."

"I was taking it slow," I said.

"That would explain it. Can I help you at all?" he asked. "I was just leaving ..."

"You're a detective?" I asked.

"I'm the office manager," he said, holding out his hand. "Wootton Fitzpaine. The detectives are Elise Liddell and Ezra Izax."

"You don't have a detective named Dodo?" I asked, prepared to be disappointed. It seemed to me like every road was leading precisely nowhere, and that *despite* me giving away Lionel's coin! So much for good luck!

"Dodo?" Wootton blinked at me. "What did you say your name was?"

"Beg your pardon," I said. "I didn't. My name is Zilla Chaplin."

"Are you ... related to Dodo?" Wootton asked, sounding more than a little unsure of himself.

"Not as far as I'm aware," I said. "Why? Is he dead?"

I'd been joking, but the look Wootton gave me suggested this wasn't a joking matter. "See for yourself," he said and moved aside so I could step past him into the office.

The first thing I noticed was how nicely furbished the place was, with clean lines, a small waiting area with soft chairs, a bookshelf and plants, and modern office furniture—apart from a rickety desk to my right and a bona fide heavy antique desk arranged centrally on the right-hand side.

The next thing I noticed was the figure slumped over the antique desk. An ancient wizard with long white curly hair and long moustaches. I recoiled, certain he was dead. Then I realised I could see his whiskers moving ...

And then I realised he was vaguely see-through.

A *ghost*? I whirled about to question Wootton, who had evidently been enjoying my various reactions.

"He's decidedly dead," Wootton told me, sounding partly regretful but mostly amused.

"Does he ... is he ... does he haunt you?" I asked.

Wootton grinned. "You don't have much experience with ghosts, I take it?"

"Absolutely none," I admitted.

Wootton indicated the far-left corner, where one of the modern desks stood. *Oh*! A ghost inhabited that one too. This one, feet up on the desk, looked like your archetypal detective, wearing a dark olive mac and with a trilby pulled over his eyes. A sudoku puzzle book with a broken spine lay face down on his desk. My mouth dropped open as I swivelled back to confront Wootton. "Are *you* real?" I whispered.

Wootton guffawed, and the ghost in the far corner wiggled in his chair before making himself more comfortable and settling down again. Wootton held out his arm. "I'm afraid I am. Nothing unusual about me at all."

I pinched his arm. Solid. "Is the other detective a ghost?" I wondered.

"No," Wootton told me. "She's flesh and blood too."

"Which is an improvement on being flesh and vodka," the ghost in the corner wearing the trilby said, without looking up. "Which is what she used to be."

"If you're looking to hire our services, I can make you an appointment for tomorrow if you like?"

Wootton offered. "Elise will be back in the office bright and early."

"I can't speak to Mr Dodo now?" I asked.

Wootton hesitated. "I'm not sure how he can help you. Dodo's a wizard, not a detective." I must have looked confused because he hastened on. "I mean, you were right in some ways. He does haunt this space. He used to live here, so he doesn't have anything to do with the detective agency as such—"

Dodo erupted. "Nincompoop!"

"Uh-oh. The Kraken awakes." Wootton folded his arms. "Be nice. There's someone here asking after you."

"What he's not telling you is that I was murdered!" the wizard bellowed. "*Murdered*!"

"And we solved the murder!" Wootton shouted back. Turning to me, he added quietly, "After a fashion."

"Wow." My head was spinning. Did I need a detective? Or a wizard? It was all too much to take in. I gripped my bag, hugging it close, and brushed at what I assumed was an annoying fly. My knees felt odd. "Do you mind if I sit down?" I asked. "I'm feeling a little giddy."

"Oh, of course, of course!" Wootton hurriedly steered me into one of the comfortable seats in the waiting area and I sat down heavily. The fly's buzzing increased and my vision greyed.

Perhaps I passed out for a moment because when the droning in my ears finally subsided, Wizard Dodo had taken the seat opposite me and Wootton was holding a glass of water out, his face softly concerned.

I accepted the glass of water and gulped at it. Icy cold. It brought me to my senses.

Whatever I had left of them.

Dodo watched me from behind round spectacles. It was difficult to read his expression, but he had kind eyes.

"I'm sorry you were murdered," I said, my voice husky.

"So am I," he agreed. "There was a lot of life left in the old dog. A lot of work to do."

"What work did you do?" I asked, taking another gulp of water.

"I was a spellkeeper. An archivist of sorts. An arcanologist of sorts. Archiving spells and hexes. All varieties. But my specialism was dark ones. Curses and the like. I would track them down and hide them away to ensure warlocks and black witches and wizards couldn't get their disgusting hands on them."

"That sounds like useful work," I said, thinking about broomstick permits.

"Unfortunately, much of it was undone ... thanks to an inept police department and my detective 'friends' here."

"That's not fair!" Wootton exclaimed. He had returned to what was presumably his desk. He'd removed his scarf too, so he must have elected to stay late at the office. That was my fault. I felt guilty again.

"I'm keeping you all," I said. "Maybe I should come back in the morning."

"Not at all," Dodo said. "The only thing you're keeping that youngster from is a pitiful stir-fry and an evening of dreadful television—"

"Who told you I was making a stir-fry tonight?" Wootton asked.

From his corner desk, the ghost detective snorted from beneath his hat. "You don't have to be a wizard to foresee what you'll have for supper. Stir-fry is all you eat. That and Chinese takeaway."

"That's true, Ezra!" Wootton said and grinned at me. "Detective Izax," he whispered before raising his voice in enthusiasm. "And pies. I love a pie. Betty's down the road sells the best pies and pasties."

"I'll remember that," I assured him.

"And ignore the old grump." Wootton indicated Dodo. "He wakes up on the wrong side of the bed every morning. Don't you, Wizard Dodo?"

I smiled at the wizard.

"Hardly," he retorted. "The dead don't sleep."

"Oh, I don't know," said Ezra from his corner. "I think you and I both do pretty well in that department."

Dodo flapped a hand in his direction, then settled his gaze on me. "Tell me, Zilla Chaplin, what brings you here?" He'd heard Wootton and I on the landing and remembered my name. Despite his grand age, he was sharp-witted, that seemed clear.

I set aside my glass of water and reached into my bag, withdrawing the grimoire and showing it to Wizard Dodo. He didn't take it from me, merely considered it with interest. "How did you come by this?"

I told him the whole sad and sorry tale. At times I attempted to cut the long story short but he would pause me and ask questions, and in the end, it seemed simpler to tell him everything. "Then the warmth of Humphrey's hands unearthed the final page, and it had the image of you and your address on it—and here I am," I finished.

"Not the *final* page," Wizard Dodo said. "There are more."

"There are?" I turned the pages gently. Every time I handled the grimoire, it became fatter, as though more information was being added to it.

And yet the pages remained confusingly blank.

"Do you know Murgatroyde Plunge?" I asked.

"I did." The wizard nodded. "A wonderfully creative witch until the events that led to her incarceration."

"Do you think she killed those children?" I asked. I didn't believe Murgatroyde was a monster, but on the other hand, what evidence was there to the contrary?

"I have no knowledge of whether she did or did not," the wizard said. "I only know the facts. Two children went missing. Only one was found. Murgatroyde was the last to see him."

I nodded. That was it. That was all anyone was working with.

"Would you like the grimoire?" I asked.

"Why in Hecate's name would I want it?"

I grunted. "I thought I'd returned it to its rightful owner, but then she disappeared. I can't comprehend how I think I saw her alive and yet her neighbour Humphrey tells me she's been dead for years."

The wizard held out a hand, and the grimoire slid from my grasp. It hovered in the air, the front page flipping open to sow dandelion clocks around the office. I watched as a butterfly rose from the pages and fluttered towards the window.

"Except Murgatroyde Plunge isn't the rightful owner," Wizard Dodo corrected me.

"It has her name in the front," I pointed out.

"I beg to differ." Dodo pushed at the air in front of the grimoire and it slipped back towards me. I hurriedly caught it before it could fall to the floor. Twisting it around, what did I see? The same writing —the gorgeous curlicues, twists and whorls that had been there before—but now, instead of the name Murgatroyde Plunge, it clearly said Zilla Chaplin.

CHAPTER EIGHTEEN

I scratched my head, staring first at the inner page of the grimoire and then at the ghost wizard. "Did you do that?" I asked suspiciously.

"I don't toy with someone else's magick," he replied, his voice grave. "Especially where the conjuring is particular."

"What does that mean? Particular?" I asked, taking the grimoire and studying my name. It looked so pretty and so permanent. As though it had always been there.

"At a guess, I would think Murgatroyde Plunge put all this in place. She wanted you to find the grimoire. She wanted you to have it. She must want you to do something for her."

"Do what?" I asked.

"All the answers you will need will be inside the grimoire," Wizard Dodo told me, sounding confident.

"But all I have in here is what I've told you about and a stack of empty pages." I quickly rifled through until I reached the page containing the image of Dodo. Flipping it over to show him the blank page overleaf, I instantly realised I'd been thwarted by the grimoire's magic. The next two pages had already filled themselves in. The background was beige, roughly stained or stamped to resemble hessian.

On the left-hand page, in thick, black, jagged letters, someone had scrawled a message.

I did not kill those children.

"Look at this!" I turned it about so the wizard could see.

Dodo smirked and sat back. "There you have it. Murgatroyde's proclamation of innocence."

Tracing the outline, I nodded. "In my gut, I think I've always known this."

"Trust your gut," Wootton piped up. "It works for me."

"You put enough rubbish into it," Dodo barked.

Feeling a little sad, I regarded the facing page.

Murgatroyde had been put away for an extraordinarily lengthy sentence if, as her—my—grimoire claimed, she hadn't committed the crime.

Eraser rubbings had been scattered all over the following page as though someone had tried to rub something out. I brushed them away. As I did so, I realised I was uncovering pencil markings etched into the background. I rubbed slightly harder. More eraser rubbings appeared. It was almost as though instead of rubbing words out, I was rubbing them into existence. Or exposing words that had once been there and had then been erased.

"The grimoire responds to *you* now. You should find it easier to reveal the messages within," Dodo told me.

"I don't understand any of this," I told him. "If it's true that she's been dead as long as people say, Murgatroyde could have had no idea of my existence. I would have been a little girl. We would never have met." But maybe we had? It was impossible to know for certain.

"So you're wondering why she chose you." Wizard Dodo nodded, considering this. "That's an interesting question ..."

I kept on smoothing the page, gently striving to

reveal faint words. *Come on, Murgatroyde*, I thought. *You might have made this a bit easier for me!*

"Perhaps she didn't choose you," the wizard mused.

I arched an eyebrow. "It doesn't feel particularly arbitrary."

"You mentioned the cat. Perhaps the cat chose you."

Blue? "That's a possibility," I agreed, secretly deciding it wasn't at all. Come on! A *cat* chose me? *Pfft*. "I did think there was a link between the cat and the grimoire at first," I admitted. "They turned up together. But Murgatroyde denied all knowledge of the cat."

"She probably lied," Dodo suggested and raised his voice so that Wootton could hear him. "In my experience, everyone does."

"Yeah, yeah," muttered Wootton, tapping away on his keyboard.

"There's also the small matter of where the grimoire has been all these years," I pointed out. "Between Murgatroyde's death and it turning up on my doorstep."

"Again, the cat may have had a hand in that," Dodo said.

"Or a paw," Wootton ventured.

Ezra, in his corner, snorted.

"But you're right. It's a mystery where her most personal effects were kept after her death," Dodo agreed.

Ezra sat up and removed his hat. He was an older gentleman with a kind face. "Presumably in her house."

"How did it find its way to Zilla then?" Wootton asked. "Are we blaming the cat for that too? The cat carried it?"

"Have you never heard of magick, Wootton?" Ezra asked, sounding despairing.

Wootton rolled his eyes, then winked at me.

"But that brings us back full circle," I said. "Why me?"

"Ezra's right. Never underestimate the power of magick," Wizard Dodo told me, as Ezra nodded sagely. "To enchant the grimoire, she wouldn't have needed to know all of the variables, only that one day someone would come along who would have the power to help her."

In my hands, the pages seemed to pulse with a life of their own, and I felt a warm, tingling sensation in my fingers.

"If Murgatroyde was half the witch I knew her to be, I have no doubt that she will have woven layers of enchantments and protections within the book, perhaps to safeguard her secrets or to guide those who seek the truth on her behalf," Dodo said.

I took a moment to process what this crazy, old, ghost of a wizard was suggesting, then giggled self-consciously. "I'm sorry to disappoint," I told everyone, "but I don't have any powers. I don't do *anything* useful except approve or deny broomstick permits. That's it."

Wizard Dodo wasn't having that. "In a world full of witches and wizards, it would be highly unusual for you not to have *anything* to bring to the table. There must be something."

"Well, if there is, I have no idea what." I tittered, continuing to brush hard at the page beneath my palm. I glanced down to see how it was going. I could read the message, no longer obscured.

I read it out loud for everyone else's benefit. "'Prove my innocence', it says, 'and I will ensure your heart's desire comes true.'"

"Wow," said Wootton.

"Interesting." Ezra nodded, leaning over his desk to smile at me.

"It may simply be that you were in the right place at the right time," Wizard Dodo surmised.

"I wish it'd been me," Wootton said, looking on enviously. "I can think of a million ways to improve my life! I'd be tearing apart every source and every piece of evidence looking for clues."

"What sources?" I asked. "Where would I look?" I didn't have the foggiest notion where to begin.

"Well ... ahm ... hmm ..." Wootton scrunched up his face.

Ezra hooted. "No detective, you, lad!" He turned to me. "I'd generally start with eye-witness statements, police reports, that kind of thing."

"But this was so long ago," I reminded him. "Surely most witnesses, if there were any, would be dead by now."

"Even the dead have plenty to say." Ezra shrugged, pointing at first himself and then Wizard Dodo. "If you're any good at tracking down ghosts."

"I doubt it," I mumbled. Until today, I'd never knowingly seen or spoken to a ghost. Unless ... Did Murgatroyde count? Had she been a ghost? But here, now, two in one day was an embarrassment of riches.

"It would help if you had a guide," Ezra agreed.

"Or a familiar who could smooth the way," Dodo suggested.

"A familiar?" I asked, thinking of Blue. "Can I just co-opt one?"

"It's best if they choose you," Wizard Dodo told me.

"Hmm." I might have to work on my cat appeal. "And then, *hey presto*! I'd have access to the right witnesses?"

Ezra grinned. "You'd still have to do a bit of work to find their location. They're usually somewhere meaningful to them. That can be where they died, but quite often it might be their old home or somewhere they had a good time."

"If I died today, I'd definitely haunt my colleagues," I said. "And not in a good way."

"A woman after my own heart," grumped Dodo.

"There are plenty of malevolent ghosts," Ezra agreed. "I've met a few of them."

"If you read old newspapers, they might indicate some useful locations," Wootton suggested. "I've done that for Elise on a few cases."

I nodded. "Good idea."

"It's a start," agreed Ezra. "Come back if you get stuck. We'll see if we can help."

"Just bear in mind this lot will charge you a fortune if you do come back," said Dodo. "Better if you ask for me instead." He preened. "After all, I am an interested party. The grimoire mentions me."

"I will," I promised, meaning 'I will' to everyone generally. I didn't intend to exclude anyone if I could help it. Ezra and Wootton had been brilliant and might prove as useful as Wizard Dodo in the future.

"Keep us updated in any case. It will be fascinating," Ezra said, "getting to the bottom of this."

"I will." I closed the grimoire and stood, thankful that my legs were no longer wobbly.

Wootton leapt up at the same time. "Will you be alright getting home? Would you care for an escort?"

I might have said yes, but Wizard Dodo jumped in before I could say anything. "She has no need of you, young rapscallion. Her friend is waiting outside."

The friend turned out to be Humphrey.

I gaped at him, surprised to see him. "What are you doing here?" Still dressed in his work clothes, he stood half in and half out of the shadows in the doorway of the tall warehouse across the lane. Closed up and in total darkness, it was a forbidding building.

"Been thinkin' 'bout ya all day, 'aven't I?"

"That's nice," I said. That pleased me more than I'd care to admit.

"Annoyin' is what it is." Humphrey sniffed before sheepishly offering me a wrinkled nose and something that may or may not have been a smile. "I wanted to make sure you was alright though."

"I'm surprised you found me," I said, jerking a thumb back towards The Hat and Dashery. "I read the number in the grimoire wrong."

"I figured that out," said Humphrey, tapping the side of his head knowingly. "I knows Tudor Lane ain't a thousand addresses long." He tipped his head back to stare up at the top floors. "But I didn't know whether you'd be in the shop or in one of them flats."

"It turns out there's a detective agency in the attic," I told him. "With some particularly obliging people." I thought about this for a second. "Well, one person and two ghosts as it happens."

"Ghosts, eh?" Humphrey raised his eyebrows.

"Have you ever had much to do with ghosts?" I asked.

"Some."

He didn't want to be especially forthcoming about this, I decided. We stood awkwardly. Humphrey dropped his gaze, watching his right foot shuffling among the leaves and rubbish that had gathered in the doorway. I wondered about his motives for turning up out of the blue. Was he lonely?

Yeah, me too, I admitted to myself.

I checked the time. "Have you had any dinner?"

He shook his head. "Came straight 'ere. Thought I might have missed ya."

"Maybe we could grab something to eat?" I suggested. It occurred to me I'd eaten nothing all day. "I passed a pub down the lane."

"The Pig and Pepper?" Humphrey shuddered. "Bit weird in there."

"Okay. Somewhere else?"

Humphrey shrugged, suddenly shy. "I'm not one for going out much."

"I'd invite you back to mine," I said, "but it's a right mess and I don't have much food in."

"You'd invite me across Celestial Street?" Humphrey looked horrified. "Oooh, that's a no from Humphrey. No no no no nooooooo."

"Why?" Wasn't he allowed to cross into Celestial Street?

My question was met with another shrug. "We could go back to my place," he said. "Although I don't have much in either."

I smiled. "Problem solved! Wootton—the young

man up in the detective agency—recommended a bakery down the road."

"Betty's." Humphrey rubbed his tummy. "'Tis renowned for the best pies."

"Who ate all the pies?" a voice asked from somewhere close by. Someone else tittered.

"Wish I 'ad!"

I grimaced. "Those Shadow People are odd," I told Humphrey. "I find them a bit unnerving."

"They has their uses."

I grunted. "If you say so. Come on. Let's go and grab ourselves a feast. My treat!"

Humphrey nodded and slipped out of the doorway. "This way."

A small queue had formed outside Betty's so we had to wait, but this only gave us extra time to gawp hungrily at the window display.

"Wow," said Humphrey, eyes wide.

"Wow indeed!" Betty's had a diverse selection of pies: everything from plain steak to all kinds of steak-and-something. There were card labels on trays of pastry-covered goodies announcing such beauties as Stilton, ale, mushroom, vegetable or even haggis. There was cheese with onion, leek, tomato or curried spinach. *Hmm.* There were fruit pies of any fruit you could imagine, and I have to say that the idea of rhubarb crumble and custard in a pie had me drooling. There were pakora pies, rabbit pies, pork pies, chicken pies, stargazy pies, fish pies, mince pies and pie pies.

Yes. Pie pies.

Don't ask.

There were also cakes, but let's not go there.

"Which to choose," Humphrey murmured beside me.

"Have anything you like," I said. The prices weren't bad compared to even the cheapest bakeries on Celestial Street. If I'd known I could get a pie here this cheaply, I'd have been visiting every lunchtime. The Ministry of Witches wasn't too far away as the crow flies. Exercise and lunch in one! I wondered if Betty's bakery offered loyalty points.

"Starter, main, dessert, whatever," I added.

Betty's was an interesting bakery. A cheerful middle-aged woman with red cheeks from the heat of the ovens served at the counter alongside a younger woman who might have been her daughter. Behind her, two men were slamming enormous wooden paddles into the vintage ovens, either sliding bread and pies in or taking them out. Meanwhile, an old woman kneaded dough at a table.

I glanced at her twice. She had that shimmery

transparency about her that I recognised from Wizard Dodo. She was a ghost too!

"What can I get you, love?" the cheerful woman asked, and I turned to Humphrey, raising a questioning eyebrow.

"Do you know what you're having?" he asked, sweetly stalling for time.

I grimaced at the woman. "I reckon I'm going to have ..." I drawled, not entirely sure until the words popped out of my mouth, "a steak and Stilton pie and a rhubarb and custard pie, please!"

"Great choices," she said, although I bet she said that to everyone. "And for you, love?"

Decision time. He spoke so quickly that the words ran together. "I'd like a cheese and bacon turnover please and a pickled herring with gherkin pie and a treacle toffee doughnut and a whisky and chocolate bonbon please and thank you."

Crikey. I reached into my bag for my purse.

It wasn't where I expected it to be. Nothing was. My heart stopped. Someone had been rummaging in my bag. Panicking, at first I couldn't find the grimoire, but then I realised that somehow it had slipped between the lining and the outer of the bag. Hiding in plain sight. How had that happened? My purse had made its way to the very bottom of the bag, which meant I hadn't had anything stolen, but the idea that someone might have been reaching for the grimoire, despite the bag being so close to my body, frightened me.

What did the grimoire contain that someone else wanted so badly?

My pies and cakes had been piled up on top of the counter in separate paper bags. With shaking hands, I extracted my card from my purse.

"Sorry, love, we only take cash," the woman told me.

Of course. This was Tumble Town. They had different rules about credit and tax. So many residents had their reasons to remain anonymous.

"That's fine," I said, knowing I had a few notes with me. I offered a twenty-pound note and received a five back, along with a handful of silver and bronze change. While Humphrey collected our purchases, I struggled to tip the coins into my purse. One odd-looking silver coin just didn't want to go. Fearing I'd been scammed with a dodgy fifty pence or something, I almost handed it back to the woman behind the counter—

But there was something familiar about it. Ignoring the queue of hungry customers behind me, I juggled my purse and bag and took a closer look.

Dusty and sticky, it had a hole in it.

Blow me if it wasn't Lionel's coin.

Like a bad penny, it had returned to me.

Huh?

It hadn't been meant for the locksmith after all.

And I still hadn't received my good luck!

CHAPTER NINETEEN

Perhaps two pies, fully loaded with deliciousness, was a step too far. After washing my hands in Humphrey's bathroom, I slumped on the sofa waiting for a fresh pot of tea to brew.

"Maybe you should 'ave a chat with Blue," Humphrey suggested, pouring the tiniest splash of milk into the waiting cups. I watched anxiously. The grimoire balanced precariously on the edge of his small coffee table and I didn't want it spattered with either milk or tea, but Humphrey had a good aim and I needn't have worried. We'd been discussing the events of the past few hours and now, with one eye on the time—I really didn't want to have to sleep on Humphrey's two-seater again; my neck and back wouldn't stand another night of cramped discomfort—we were discussing next steps.

"Have you ever owned a familiar?" I asked.

"I'm not a witch," he reminded me. "An' besides, I'm not sure you ever do *own* 'em."

His words echoed around me as I picked up the delicate porcelain cup, its warmth seeping into my fingers. The aroma of the tea was comforting, a stark contrast to the tumultuous thoughts in my mind. Humphrey's suggestion lingered. Blue seemed to be, if not *the* key, then at least one of them. Could the cat help unravel this mystery? And how would I approach a conversation with a familiar? The mere idea felt foreign yet intriguing.

"I don't know much about familiars," I admitted. "We did some work with them at school but I've never had one. I'm allergic to cats and some dogs. It wouldn't have occurred to me to try any other type of creature."

"Now's yer chance!" Humphrey, obviously full of bon viveur and conviviality, crossed his legs like a yogi beneath his slim frame, almost disappearing into his floompfy armchair. He looked a little incongruous, still in his work trousers and shirt.

"How do I ... converse with a cat?" I asked.

Humphrey tutted. “The same way you do with anyone, I suppose.”

“Mmm.” That made sense when you thought about it. “I’ll give it a go if I ever see him again.”

Humphrey tittered. “You are funny, Zilla. Don’t just talk to him. I reckon if you want to get him onside, yer gonna have to bond with ’im. Show ’im some respect. It seems to me Blue’s more than a cat. There’s somethin’ else there. Wisdom and experience. I should think he’s seen a few things we can’t even imagine.”

I considered this, sipping my tea thoughtfully. “So, I should treat him like an equal?”

“Exackly! Let ’im come to you. Be patient. He’ll turn up when the time’s right, then you just need to approach him with an open mind.”

This had been quite a conversation for Humphrey. He flushed and hid his face behind his cup. “That’s what I’d do, anyhoo.”

I nodded, feeling a little more confident but still unsure. The thought of forming a bond with a familiar was daunting yet exciting. Blue seemed to be the only one who could shed light on the peculiar events we were entangled in. But he was a cat, and cats don’t speak.

"Alright," I said. "I'll keep my eyes open for him. Maybe he'll show up when I least expect it."

Humphrey peeped out from behind his cup.

I held my own out and clinked his cup against mine in a toast. "To unexpected allies and the mysteries they help solve," I said.

As we finished our tea, the room seemed to grow warmer, the air charged with a sense of possibility. I knew that the path ahead wouldn't be easy, but I felt oddly reassured to have Humphrey as a friend along with—hopefully—Blue's potential insight.

"I ought to be going," I said, and I felt Humphrey slump in his seat. I hurried to reassure him. "I'm not going to work tomorrow. Can I pop around when you get home?"

He cheered up instantly. "If ya like," he said, playing it cool.

He wasn't fooling me. Humphrey enjoyed having a friend as much as I did.

"What you gonna do tomorrow?" he asked.

"I want to have a closer look at the newspaper reports from the time Socrates and Greta disappeared to see if there are any potential witnesses I could talk to. Even if they are dead ones." I laughed nervously. "Of course, *that's* another reason I need to find Blue." I met Humphrey's gaze. "It's crazy, isn't it? Needing a cat to speak to ghosts?"

"I s'pose it don't have to be a cat." Humphrey shrugged. "But don't suppose you has any other contenders, do ya?"

"No." I picked up the grimoire from the coffee table and smoothed the cover. I experienced a now familiar tingling of energy beneath my palm. "This thing is incredible," I told him. "So full of life."

"Revealin' its secrets as it chooses," Humphrey agreed. "You need to keep it safe."

I nodded, feeling the weight of responsibility. "I will." A promise to him, to myself and to the grimoire as I slipped it into my bag. "And thanks, Humphrey. For everything."

He flashed a rare, genuine smile, his cheeks pink. "Don't mention it. Good luck with the ghosts and the cat."

"I'll come over tomorrow and fill you in with all the details," I promised.

"You sure you don't want me to walk ya back to Celestial Street?" he asked, untangling his legs so that he could stand and see me out.

"I'll be fine."

"Mind 'ow you go, now."

With that, I bade him farewell and stepped out

into the cool, drizzly evening air, my mind whirling with plans and possibilities. The street lights cast long shadows on the narrow pavement, and I shivered, not just with cold but in anticipation. Tomorrow was another day, another chance to uncover some long-buried secrets.

But first I had to get home.

I turned to wave to Humphrey but he'd already hurried back inside.

"Sensible," I muttered, starting for home along Fire Beacon Lane.

A few minutes later I passed the burial place and paused, scanning the consecrated ground—not that I could see much, not in the darkness. The only light here spilled from the lamps in the cobbled circular area—Marlene Court as it was known locally, according to Humphrey—in front of the craft shop. The two small dwellings that faced the burial place were in darkness. I made a mental note to see whether I could track down the people who had lived there at the time of the murder.

What had the residents seen or heard? Had they been invited to give evidence at the trial?

Water trickled down a nearby drainpipe. The drizzle had turned to light rain. Pulling the hood of my cloak down over my face a little more, I resumed my trek home. I hadn't gone far when I heard soft footsteps.

I paused, suddenly hyper alert.

Other people are allowed to walk the streets, I reminded myself.

"Hide." A whisper from beside me.

I jerked my head to the right. No-one there. A shadow person.

"Hide." More imperative.

The footsteps were coming closer. I cocked my head, nervously licking my lips. Someone ahead of me, but I wasn't sure which path. Directly ahead? Diagonally to the right? Or right?

Just because someone is out and about after dark, it doesn't mean they're after me!

I stepped back, out of the light. Somewhere behind me, back down Fire Beacon Lane, a dog barked.

Someone walking their dog, that's all.

"*Hide*!" The whisper was savage now.

I dashed back to the burial place and slid in through the gate. If I could make it to the rear corner where the craft shop's back wall met its neighbour's side wall, I could hunker down among the gravestones.

The ground was soft and boggy, as if it had

recently been turned over. The thought made me wince. I didn't want to come face to face with parts of a skeleton, but this was not the time to be squeamish. I threw myself behind a tall stone statue, clutched my bag tightly and drew my knees to my chest.

Breathe, I told myself. *Just do it quietly!*

The footsteps grew louder, echoing through the night air with a menacing cadence. I pressed myself harder against the cold stone of the statue, feeling its rough texture dig into my back. The hairs on my neck prickled in alarm, and I strained my eyes and ears to catch any hint of movement.

A shadow flitted across the path, quick and elusive, like a phantom. My heart pounded in my chest, each beat resounding in my ears like a drum. The whisper had been right; someone was out there, and they were closing in.

I dared to peek around the edge of the statue, my eyes wide with fear. A figure emerged from the darkness, moving with purpose. They paused, looking around as if searching for something—or someone.

It might not be me! It might not be me!

The moonlight cast a ghostly glow on their face, revealing sharp features and a grim expression.

Panic surged through me, and I bit my lip to keep

from making a sound. If it *was* me they were after, if they knew I was hiding here, if they found me ...

I couldn't finish the thought. I had to stay hidden, had to remain silent.

The figure continued their search, turning their head from side to side, raking the area, much as I had a few minutes before. I held my breath, every muscle in my body tense and ready to flee. They took a step closer to my hiding spot, and I could see the gleam of something metallic in their hand. My mind raced with possibilities—was it a weapon? A flashlight?

Suddenly, the dog barked again, louder and more insistent. The figure froze, then turned and hurried off towards Marlene Court. I exhaled shakily, relief flooding through me as I watched them disappear into the night.

I stayed crouched behind the statue for what felt like hours but was probably only a few minutes, my ears tuned to any hint of danger. When I was sure the coast was clear, I slowly uncurled my limbs and stepped out from my hiding place. I needed to get away.

To get home.

Cautiously, I edged to the end of the lane, hogging the shadows.

But then—

No!

Male voices.

I pressed myself against the damp brick of the craft shop and held my breath.

"She must have passed you," the first voice said accusingly.

She? This didn't sound promising.

"I'm telling you, she didn't. *You* lost her." The second voice sounded annoyed.

"I was waiting for her outside that creature's house. I followed her from there."

That creature? If they were referring to Humphrey, then they definitely meant me!

"If you'd had eyes on her the whole time, you'd have seen which way she went!" the second voice hissed.

The dog barked again. Closer than before. It sounded lonely. Probably a stray. What if it wandered down here and barked at me? It would give the game away. I needed to make a move.

"There was nowhere she could have gone. She was on her way home so she must have passed you!"

"No, she must have taken a different route," the first voice decided. "Why don't you go back up that way and I'll go this way."

This way? I inched away from the wall, straining

to see the figures. I could make out the back of one. He pointed up the diagonal. Would the other one be coming back down here? I dithered, unsure whether to dive back into my hiding place or remain where I was.

Boots slithered on the cobblestones, sounding altogether too close for comfort. My heart, until now beating like a gong, threatened to stop altogether.

But the footsteps faded away.

Thank you, thank you!

With no time to lose, I darted out from my hiding place. I couldn't go straight on as that would be my normal route, and I couldn't go along the diagonal as the first man had disappeared up there, so I had to go left or right or back.

Back might have been the safest option—that's where Humphrey was, after all. I could wait out the night in his house, but for some stupid reason I was intent on getting home.

Running out of time, I took the left turn.

The path was narrower here, and the buildings leaning in above my head cast deep, impenetrable shadows, seeming to conspire to keep me hidden. I pressed on, my careful footsteps a soft sigh against the stones except where I slid on greasy cobbles. The night was a conspirator now, wrapping me in its inky embrace, but whose side it was on—mine or my would-be assailants?

I could hear the distant murmur of the river, its fast flow a stark contrast to the pounding in my ears. A flicker of movement ahead caught my eye, and I pulled up, my breath catching in my throat. But it was only a cat, a black cat, its eyes glowing like twin moons as it slunk into a doorway.

I hesitated. I didn't want to venture any closer to the river! Deadman's Wharf at this time of night? Surely it would be a no-go area. I took the first turning I came to. Right. Then the next right. Every turning steered me into another narrow alley, some barely wide enough for one person to walk, others a little wider, where the dwellings stood respectfully back from each other.

I quickened my pace, each step leading me deeper into unfamiliar territory. The houses and tiny shops here were older, their façades crumbling, a testament to a time long past. I could see the flickering light of a lantern in a window up ahead. Hope surged within me.

Suddenly, a voice rang out, sharp and urgent. I ducked into the nearest doorway, cramming my fist against my mouth. The voices were closer now, and I could make out the words, muffled but filled with intent. The same men, still searching for me, their determination palpable.

I had to keep moving. I darted from my hiding place, keeping to the darkest part of the alley, and made my way towards the end of this lane. The next turn led me to a small passageway, more than likely a shortcut for locals. But I wasn't a local and my head compass had imploded. I was completely lost, but this thin ribbon between the buildings was probably my best chance of slipping away unnoticed.

As I reached the corner, I glanced back, scouring the darkness for any sign of pursuit. The lane behind me was empty, the shadows concealing my passage. I took a deep breath, steeling myself for the horror of the dark before me.

Dare I turn on the torch on my phone? I hadn't gone more than a few feet and I knew I would have to. This alleyway was narrow but also cluttered with debris: bins, bags of rubbish, discarded household goods. I couldn't move without tripping over. Shielding the glare of the torch as best I could, I navigated the twists and turns, picking up my feet, focusing on the goal: the bright lights of Celestial Street. Home would be just beyond there. I could almost feel its warmth, its safety.

I heard the clattering of a dustbin lid behind me.

Fumbling with my phone, I turned the light off and, gritting my teeth, skirted around a final pile of rubbish.

Emerging from the alley, I saw welcoming lights. Cutting across Tumble Town, Cross Lane ran from Celestial Street all the way down to Deadman's Wharf and the Thames. Relief washed over me, and for the first time, I allowed myself to believe that I might make it.

Without looking behind me, I bolted up the lane and burst through into Celestial Street, bustling with shoppers even at this time of night. I dived among them, dodging this way and that, hoping I'd lose any pursuer among all the other similarly attired cloak-clad witches and wizards. Of course, my pursuers knew full well I'd be going home, but if I could get there before them ...

Once clear of Celestial Street, ruing the amount of pie I'd finished off at Humphrey's place, I ran, clasping my bag tight against my chest, splashing through puddles, struggling to breathe. My hood dislodged from my head, bouncing around my shoulders, but finally, as the rain beat down, City View Court hove into view.

On the verge of tears, I threw myself inside the communal lobby and took the stairs two at a time, slamming myself against my newly refurbished front door.

Made it!

But just as I was about to unlock it, a hand clamped down on my shoulder.

I jumped a mile and screeched, rounding on the owner of the hand, ready to beat whoever it was to death with the grimoire if necessary. "Get back!" I screamed. "*Get back*!"

CHAPTER TWENTY

"Get away from me!" I jerked backwards, fearing for my life.

But there was no need.

It was only Mr Redhill from Flat 6.

Cowering away from me, he regarded me with horrified curiosity. "Are you alright?" he asked. "You look terribly pale."

I laughed weakly, one hand clutching my bag, the other my chest. "I had a bit of a scare," I told him. "But I'm okay now." I reached into my sodden bag, searching for my keys.

"Would you like me to hold anything?" he asked.

"No, thank you," I panted. "I can manage."

Locating the new key, I turned away from him

and shoved it into the shiny new lock. It went in like a knife through butter. I thought my knees might give way through sheer relief. I'd made it.

"Sorry, Mr Redhill," I said, turning back to him. "Did you need something?"

"No, no, not at all." He smiled and held his hands palm up. "I heard you'd had a bit of trouble and I've popped by a few times today to see if there was anything I could do. But obviously you've been out." He tilted his head, his eyes wandering to the bag I held in my hand. "At work or something."

"It's kind of you to check up on me," I told him. "I had a break-in."

"Oh, no!" Mr Redhill commiserated. "I hope nothing valuable was taken."

"I don't own anything of value," I told him. "Even my laptop is retro. They made a lot of mess and that's about it."

"I suppose that's something. If you need any help—?"

"It's all in hand, thanks."

"Alright then. I'd best leave you to it." He hesitated. "You're very damp."

I shivered. "And cold."

"Would you like to come up for a cup of tea?" he offered. "It might help warm you up."

I hesitated, glancing at the door and then back at him. The idea of a hot drink was tempting, but I wanted to get inside and lock my door. "Not this time," I said finally, giving him a small smile. "But thanks."

"Not at all," he said, waving a hand dismissively. "I just wanted to make sure you were alright. A break-in can be extremely unsettling."

"It was," I admitted. "But I'll be okay. It's just ... a lot to process."

He nodded understandingly. "Take your time. If you need anything, you know where to find me."

"Thanks," I said again, grateful for his kindness.

I watched him walk away and climb the stairs. Once his head had disappeared and he could no longer see me, I breathed a sigh of relief and pushed open my front door, reaching to flick on the hall light. The flat was exactly as I'd left it: quiet and heavily scented with floral surface cleaner. I dumped my robes on the kitchen floor and extracted the grimoire from my bag. Clutching it tightly under one arm, I filled the kettle and switched it on, intending to make myself some chamomile and lavender tea.

While the kettle boiled, I wandered into the living room but didn't turn the lights on. Instead, I loitered by the window, staring out. I could see the rain in the circle of light thrown by the street lamps.

Scanning the doorways, I watched and waited. If I stood here long enough, would I see one of the men who'd been chasing me through Tumble Town? Would they loiter in a doorway all night, hoping I'd break cover so they could catch me?

Except ... it wasn't me they were after, was it?

I was nothing.

The only thing in my life that had changed lately was that I'd become the somewhat nervous owner of Murgatroyde's grimoire.

It *had* to be the grimoire they wanted.

Holding it in both hands, I surveyed the cover before flipping to the first page. Even in the dark of my living room, I could see my name was still there. What would happen if someone stole the grimoire from me? Would their name appear on the title page instead?

And what exactly was inside that made it worth stealing?

The kettle whistled, breaking my reverie. I tore myself away from the window and returned to the kitchen, my mind still spinning with questions. As I poured the steaming water over the teabag, the scent of chamomile and lavender mixed with the lingering floral cleaner created a strangely calming atmosphere.

I headed for bed, settling in with my tea and the grimoire, feeling the weight of its secrets. Carefully, I turned each of the completed pages, scanning for any clues that might reveal my next move.

I'd intended to slip the grimoire under my mattress before I fell asleep, but the tea worked its magick and my eyes closed of their own volition.

I didn't hear the grimoire as it slipped from the duvet and onto the floor.

I awoke in a panic with the dawn.

I'd been dreaming about endless passageways and alleys, a perfect labyrinth with no exit. Something dark—little more than a black cloud that I'd glimpsed out of the corner of my eye—had been following me. I knew I needed to get to safety but couldn't figure out a way. My anxiety had been mounting, and now I opened my eyes and jerked up, clutching my throat and struggling to breathe.

The grimoire! What had I done with it?

My heart raced as I scanned the room. Not on the bed. Not on the bedside table. In a panic, I leaned over to scour the floor and spotted it half under the bed, the pages still closed. Phew! Feeling relieved, I reached down and picked it up, the simple act of holding it helping to soothe my frayed nerves.

"Sorry," I told the old book. "I should have been more careful." Smoothing the front cover, I opened the grimoire to the meadow page. Watching the grass and flowers spring forth and the butterflies dance in the air brought me a serene joy I'd never experienced before.

This was sensational magick.

I didn't understand it, not for one minute. Murgatroyde Plunge must have been an incredible witch—and artist! A proper creative soul—to pull this off. I flipped through the pages until I found her protestation of innocence.

I did not kill those children.

"I believe you, Murgatroyde," I said, gently stroking the letters. "I'll do everything I can to help you."

As I muttered the words, a soft glow radiated from the grimoire, causing my fingers to tingle and eventually enveloping my hand in a warm, reassuring light.

I knew I couldn't stay tucked up in bed forever. Murgatroyde's secrets didn't lie between my sheets. In any case, the grimoire had to be protected, and so did I. My dreams had indicated that danger was closing in, and I needed to remain one step ahead. I showered and drank a glass of water, then, with the grimoire safely tucked into my backpack, I decided to leave, heading towards the one place I could think of where I might find answers—the old library in the bowels of the Ministry of Witches. I knew from hanging out there from time to time while I'd studied for my degree that it housed ancient tomes, old newspapers, letters, parish and council records and registers, and mysteries long forgotten.

The streets were quiet as I walked briskly, the early morning mist curling around my feet like ethereal tendrils. There were folk out and about, but Celestial Street itself would remain slumbering for another few hours. Witches and wizards are mainly nocturnal creatures, and business hours tended to reflect this. I kept a careful eye on anyone who crossed my path, seeing danger everywhere. Meanwhile, my mind was already racing ahead, pondering on possible discoveries.

I needed a break. Something that would shed

more light on who had—assuming it wasn't Murgatroyde—killed the children.

Arriving at the imposing stone steps of the Ministry of Witches, I took a deep breath and ventured inside. The air, as always, was thick with the scent of old parchment and ink, and the faint hum of soft voices resonated through the hallways. I navigated the labyrinthine corridors to the back of the building and took the stairs down and down and down again until I reached the entrance to the library, open twenty-four hours a day for scholars, journalists, researchers and writers alike.

The ancient oak doors towered above me, always a formidable sight. I experienced a thrill of excitement as I always had when I'd visited years before. Pushing the doors open, the familiar sight of endless rows of bookshelves greeted me, each crammed with volumes of magickal knowledge. One of the librarians, an elderly witch with grey hair piled on her head and spectacles perched on the end of her nose, glanced up and nodded at me. I returned the gesture and made my way to a secluded corner of the library, where the dust seemed to settle more heavily and the creaking bookshelves and scrape of heavy wooden chairs whispered of forgotten lore.

Setting the grimoire on a large wooden table, I

carefully opened it once more. The pages pulsed with a life of their own, and I felt the tingling sensation in my fingers again. I re-read every single word of what was written, scanning the illustrations for anything I might have missed. There was nothing. Finally, I turned over to the first pair of blank sheets and glared at them.

If my will alone could have written words across there, the words would have sung from the pages. Sadly, nothing new was forthcoming. Instead I tried sliding my palms, warming the fibres of the old paper. Again, the pages remained blank.

You're going to have to help me out here, Murgatroyde!

"Maybe you should try using a pen."

I jumped. I hadn't realised anyone had ventured close to my table. It was the librarian who'd greeted me on my way inside the library. Wearing the familiar Ministry of Witches robes over an ankle-skimming black dress, she hugged a pile of books under one arm, waving her spectacles in her other hand.

I smiled. "I don't think it's that easy." I whispered because it was a library but also because I didn't want to attract any other unwanted attention.

"It usually is," the librarian whispered back and popped her specs on. "Do you have a pen?"

Before I could answer—I did have several in my backpack—she handed me one of her own. "Try this," she instructed me and, pulling a book from her pile, set about searching the bookshelves for the correct place to shelve it.

Left to my own devices, I stared at the pen—a black fountain pen with silver trimming—and then at the blank page. Should I mark the grimoire?

Why not? It belongs to me now.

But what if I'm writing over something important? Something that Murgatroyde intends to reveal to me in the future?

I hesitated, the pen hovering just above the aged parchment, the ink glistening ominously on the nib. Taking a deep breath, I pressed the pen down. *I don't know what to write*, I wrote. The ink flowed smoothly, etching elegant swirls and lines onto the page.

This didn't resemble my scruffy handwriting at all. I tried again. *What should I write?* The handwriting was gorgeous, confident. Then, to my astonishment, as soon as the ink dried, the letters started to shift and rearrange themselves, forming new words, then whole sentences. Slowly, a message became visible.

Welcome, Zilla, Keeper of the Grimoire. Your journey begins now.

The words shimmered briefly before settling onto the page. My heart raced with a mixture of excitement and trepidation.

I glanced around to see if anyone had noticed the magickal display, but the librarian had moved on to a different section, her back turned to me. Taking another deep breath, I continued writing, compelled by a power beyond my comprehension. However, if I expected the page to fill with instructions and arcane symbols, guiding me through the first steps of unlocking the grimoire's secrets, I was disappointed.

Instead, a list presented itself. I cocked my head, watching as the letters swirled around the page, tangling and untangling themselves before finally settling down into words.

To-do list.

To-do list? Was it kidding me? This was like being back at work!

Except it wasn't. Not really. There, my ordinary to-do lists were the same every day and were as exciting as watching paint dry. This one, in the grimoire, didn't even make sense!

The Spookiest of the Spooks

The Direst of the Diabolical

The Gravest of Gravestones

The Grimmest of Grimoires

Come on, Murgatroyde! Give me just a smidgen more, I silently pleaded and returned the pen to the page. It paused there for what seemed an age before finally scratching out a series of lines, circles and symbols before the whole cycle of scrambling letters began again.

Find.

Find.

Find.

Find.

Over and over, that one word appeared until I gently touched the page with my left hand. "Okay," I whispered, "Okay. I will. But—"

The pen whipped left and right of its own accord, moving so quickly it smudged its own marks.

Greta. Greta. Where is Greta?

"Where is Greta?" I spoke the words out loud.

"Ssssh!" A hiss from behind me. I glanced over my shoulder, worried someone was watching me, but I couldn't see anyone, and the librarian who had loaned me the pen had disappeared.

The pen underlined the word 'where' half a dozen times.

"What do you mean?" I whispered. "Where's her ... body?"

No no no nobody nobody nobody knows know-body nos no-one knows what I no—

The fountain pen spat words like bullets.

I lowered my voice even more, so quiet that I was almost speaking under my breath, my mouth forming words that nobody else could hear. "What do you know?"

Didn't die didn't die didn't die not there not then not there

I frowned at the words on the page, my heart thudding in my chest. "Where is she then?" I pressed.

The pen hesitated, then set about scribbling again, slower this time, as though trying to convey something crucial.

Find her find her find her follow the signs—

"Signs?" I whispered. "What signs?"

Look look look and you will see you will see if you look look see—

Abruptly, the pen stopped moving and the ink flow ceased. I sat back, feeling a mixture of dread and curiosity. The silence of the library enveloped me, broken only by the faint rustling of pages from distant corners.

I peered around, hoping to find some inspiration.

A few tables along from me, someone was reading today's paper. I could see the sports headline: *West Tumble Town Wizards tumble to bottom of table!*

How dull, I thought.

But the newspaper reminded me of the stored-on microfilm here in the archive. I gently closed the grimoire and packed it into my backpack. What should I do with the pen? I searched among the stacks for a few minutes and at the main desk, but the witch with the spectacles was nowhere to be seen.

I jammed it in my pocket instead—praying it wouldn't leak—and went in search of the microfilm readers. There were half a dozen of them, housed in small open cubicles lined up against a wall. Two were occupied, so I chose one at the end, out of view of anyone who might sneak up on me. They were the old-fashioned type. You had to loop the film through the machine, making sure to catch the end securely, and then use a handle to wind the film through.

All I needed now were the right films for the newspapers from 20 March 1958 and the few days after Socrates had been killed in Fire Beacon Lane's burial place. I retrieved half a dozen rolls of film, opened the grimoire and a notebook, and began to search.

The early edition of *The Celestial Times* had scant detail. It simply stated that two children had been reported missing the previous evening and that a body had been found. Next of kin had been informed.

The later version was a different story.

It described the scene in grim detail, noting some peculiar symbols etched into the earth around the body and the 'air of mystery that seemed to cloak the entire area'. The police had cordoned off Fire Beacon Lane, and whispers about an evil child killer had begun to spread through Tumble Town like wildfire.

The news report for the next day had even more detail—including the autopsy. This was information I'd never come across before. Socrates had died from a head injury. His skull had been cracked like an egg.

I frowned.

Forensics had been in their infancy back in the day. While the detectives involved in the case would almost certainly have searched among the grave markers for clues—shoeprints, lost items, cigarette butts, a weapon, that kind of thing, would they have had a pathologist involved who would have also been seeking evidence of an accident?

For example, was it feasible that Socrates had fallen and caught his head on a gravestone?

I noted the name of the detective in charge of the case. Detective Sergeant William Larch. He would be one of the ghosts worth talking to, as Ezra had suggested. In fact, perhaps Ezra would make a good go-between. If he could call on DS Larch in the afterlife, maybe he could introduce me to him. That would be a huge help and would negate the immediate need to find Blue.

But even if Socrates had died following an accident, that didn't explain what had happened to Greta.

Unless ...

Unless ...

I hardly dared think the thought, but ... what if Greta had been responsible for her brother's death? She might have run away, afraid of the consequences.

But an eleven-year-old child can't exist on the streets for long. She might have remained in hiding for a while. Perhaps someone had taken her in. But how had she never shown up subsequently? How long had the police searched for her? When had they given up?

The papers of the time provided no further answers to this mystery, but I spent a little more time studying the black-and-white photos that illustrated the stories. There was a photo of DS Larch addressing journalists. And photos of the children. There were photos of the burial place, the grass, bushes and mud heavily trampled, and a photo of a neighbour who'd been interviewed for *The Tumble Town Tribune*, a paper I'd never heard of.

A neighbour?

I skimmed the accompanying article for a name. *There*! Mr K Barber. He claimed that children had been making a nuisance of themselves playing in the burial place late at night, disturbing him when he went to bed.

If that was the case, then Mr K Barber must have lived in one of the small dwellings directly across from the crime scene and would be another brilliant witness worth speaking to. I wrote down his name in my notebook.

I studied the images of Socrates and Greta one final time. Socrates had a wide smile and was missing a few teeth. His dark hair had been flipped over his head from a side parting so that his fringe hung down above one eye.

Greta had a thinner face and a more reserved smile, her mouth only slightly open in her photograph, showing a gap between her two top front teeth. Her hair had a kink to it and was lighter than Socrates', but given the black-and-white photograph, I didn't know what shade.

A young library assistant chose to stroll directly behind me at that moment and, on a whim, I caught his attention. "Excuse me," I said. "Do you know if there's any way to get clearer copies of these photographs?"

"I mean, we can arrange photocopies." He leaned over and took a closer look. "*The Tumble Town Tribune*, is it?"

I nodded.

"As it happens, that title is now defunct—"

"Oh."

"But we have their archive, original copies of the newspaper as well, of course—"

"They might be clearer, mightn't they?"

"Chances are we still have their original photographs too."

The news took a moment to sink in, until, "Really?" I squeaked a little too loudly. A couple of my fellow readers turned to judge me.

"If you take a note of the details—paper, page, column, etcetera—you can request the photos to come out to you from the archive. Just speak to a librarian at the desk."

"Ooh! I will," I whispered. "Thanks!"

"No problem."

I did as he suggested and made my way over to the counter to fill in a request form. The no-nonsense librarian on duty there dealt with me briskly.

"It will be ten to twenty minutes," she told me. "Take a seat and I'll find you."

I installed myself in a quiet corner of the library, letting the anticipation build as I waited for the librarian to return with the photographs. My mind raced with the possibilities of what I might discover in those old images. Could they hold the key to unlocking Murgatroyde's mystery?

After what felt like an eternity, the librarian reappeared, carrying a thick old cardboard box labelled by hand with the archive details I had given her. She placed it carefully on the table in front of me and left me to my work with a nod.

I opened the box and found not only the four images I'd requested—both school photographs of the children and two images of the burial place taken by the Tribune's photographer, one Zorba Arvanataki—but a bunch of others that had been taken on the same reel by the same photographer. The date on the reverse was the very same day Socrates' body had been found. I gingerly pulled out the photographs, each a snapshot of history frozen in time. As I studied them, I felt a shiver of excitement run down my spine. There, in the grainy black-and-white images, were faces and places that seemed to whisper secrets across the decades.

I flipped the image of Socrates over. This had been labelled—again by hand—as a copy from a negative provided by his foster parents. The same with Greta's. I still couldn't tell what colour Greta's eyes and hair were, but now I could see the freckles on her nose and tell that her skin was pale.

Would I be able to take copies of these? Or ... Glancing around, I whipped out my mobile phone and hurriedly snapped close-ups of Socrates, Greta, DS Larch and Mr Barber. Then, because I'd managed to get away with doing that, I snapped the scene of crime photos too, before hurriedly replacing everything neatly inside the box.

I shut the folder, feeling the weight of the mystery settle more heavily on my shoulders. The questions seemed endless, each answer leading to more perplexities. Determined to get to the bottom of it, I decided that Mr K Barber was my next lead.

I gathered my things, ensuring that the grimoire was tucked safely at the bottom of my bag, and picked up the archive box to return to the counter. The pen-lending librarian had finished shelving and had taken up her duty behind the desk. I handed over the box and fished in my pocket for her fountain pen.

"Thank you for the loan of the pen," I said.

"Pen?" she asked, seeming genuinely puzzled.

"Yes." I held it out.

"I've never seen that before. You'd better keep it."

"But you—"

She interrupted me. "Did you find everything you needed today?"

"It's been a productive few hours." More like six hours, I realised. Wow.

She regarded me with a knowing smile.

"See? Sometimes it *is* that easy," she said softly before gliding away, leaving me holding the pen out in thin air. I considered leaving it for her on the desk —it was a fountain pen, after all, and they're not cheap!—but something told me she knew precisely what she was doing.

She wanted me to have it.

As I left the library, the sun had begun its descent, casting long, eerie shadows across the cobblestone streets. The flicker of hope I had felt earlier surged stronger within me. There was a sense of urgency now, a need to uncover the truth and bring closure to the mystery that had haunted this town for so long.

Time to head back to Wonderland Detective Agency and have another word with Ezra.

CHAPTER TWENTY-ONE

It struck me as I headed along Cross Lane that I'd spent more time in Tumble Town over the past few days than I had in my entire life. I wasn't over my fear of the place—not at all—but perhaps I was getting accustomed to the peculiarities of its narrow lanes and alleys, the buildings leaning in as if to whisper conspiratorially to each other, the cloaked figures who avoided your eye, not to mention the mightily weird whispers in the shadows.

Yes ... perhaps.

The sun had dipped below the horizon by the time I reached 125 Tudor Lane, the sky—what I could see of it—now painted in hues of indigo and violet. I paused at the entrance to the side of The Hat and Dashery, taking a deep breath, steeling myself for what came next. Pushing open the door and walking into the entry, I was greeted by the creaking of the wooden floorboards and the faint hot scent of a steaming iron.

At the top of the stairs, I knocked on the office door and walked inside. Wizard Dodo was asleep at his desk and there was no sign this evening of Wootton or Elise, but Ezra was waiting for me, his translucent frame—wallowing in his chair—silhouetted against the dim light of the office. He looked up as I entered, his eyes narrowing with curiosity. "You look like you've seen a ghost," he remarked, his voice tinged with amusement.

"Ha!"

"I've been expecting you," he said.

"You have?" I couldn't recall giving him any hint I'd be returning today.

He indicated the chair opposite his. "I imagine you have lots of questions."

I snuck a look at Wizard Dodo, slumbering peacefully. Would he want to be part of this?

"Don't worry about him," Ezra said. "We'll wake him if we need to, but it's usually best to let sleeping wizards lie, I find."

I nodded and plopped into the spare chair.

"What can I do for you?" Ezra asked, leaning

back, a tatty folded notebook in one hand and a stub of a pencil in the other.

"I've been going back through the newspaper articles of the time—"

"You've found them helpful?"

"Some. There's a lot of sensationalism."

"Mmm."

"But I found the name of a witness I'd like to speak to ..." I rummaged in my bag and extracted my notebook. "Mr K someone or other. Oh, there it is. Mr K Barber." I glanced across at Ezra, but he showed no sign of recognition at the name. No reason why he should. "The other name on my list—"

"It's a short list—" Ezra remarked, winking.

"I'll add to it!" I promised. "The lead detective on Murgatroyde's case was DS William Larch."

"Ah!" Ezra raised his eyebrows.

"You know him?"

Ezra shifted in his seat. "Bill Larch. I knew him but only vaguely. He was retiring as I joined the force. He looked like a throwback to the 1930s, never mind the fifties. Always wearing a dapper suit and a trilby." He laughed and pointed at his own. "Maybe he was something of a style guru. Whatever, he *was* a legend among the chaps who'd been there a while."

He pursed his lips and thought back before adding, "I never quite bought into him. Not totally. He'd had a few successes, and I do think he capitalised on a couple of his more infamous cases, but ..."

"But?"

"But," Ezra continued, "there were whispers that he tended to embellish his reports. Not outright lies, you understand, but he liked to paint a picture, to create a narrative that was perhaps slightly more dramatic than the reality."

I tilted my head, curious. "Embellish how?"

Ezra shrugged. "Oh, little things. Adding a spot of flair to his descriptions, making his role seem more central than it might have been. Nothing that would compromise a case, but enough to make him a bit of a character. Someone his colleagues might look up to and admire."

I nodded, making a mental note to dig deeper into Larch's cases. If there was a hint of truth to these whispers, it could either complicate or simplify my search for the truth about Murgatroyde.

"Interesting," I said. "Do you think it would be worth tracking him down for an interview?"

Ezra raised one eyebrow, nodding knowingly. "As a ghost, you mean? Because there's no way he's still alive."

"That's what I thought."

"If he can be found, he might be worth talking to. Retired detectives are prone to either fade into obscurity or become very chatty, especially with someone interested in their glory days. Retired ghost detectives are even worse."

I grinned at that. "Well, I'd like to try."

"Give me your number. I'll ask around and see if anyone knows if he's active."

Active as a ghost. My mind boggled. Broomstick permits seemed a million miles away.

I recited my number, watching as he carefully wrote it down in his notebook before depositing that and his stubby pencil into his coat pocket. The street lights outside flickered on, casting fleeting shadows across the office. Ezra had never appeared more spectral than at that moment.

"Do you think Larch would be willing to talk about Murgatroyde specifically?" I asked, my curiosity getting the better of me.

Ezra hesitated for a moment before responding. "Hard to say. If he's still holding on to his old bravado, he may well jump at the chance to share his stories. But ghosts ... I'm sorry to admit, they can be unpredictable." He nodded towards the sleeping

Wizard Dodo. "They might remember things differently, or not at all."

I pondered his words, considering the implications of dealing with a ghost who might embellish or forget crucial details. It was a risk, but one I would have to take. The truth about Murgatroyde was worth it.

"Alright," I said. "Let's see what we can find out. Thanks, Ezra."

He tipped his hat slightly in response, a gesture that seemed to echo the bygone era Larch had reportedly embodied.

I crept past Wizard Dodo and made my way outside.

CHAPTER TWENTY-TWO

Electing to wear my backpack on my chest—making it a frontpack that I could protect with my arms—I took special care as I navigated the narrow lanes and alleys on my way to Humphrey's place. Now and then I would pause and listen, checking for footsteps. Occasionally I would dart into a side passage or a deep doorway to wait, watching to see if anyone was following me.

I glared at anyone who came near me, sending out the meanest vibes I could. *Stay away!* I'd telegraph. *Stay right away or I'll practise some of my badly neglected defensive magick on you.*

Maybe I was being ridiculous, but it paid to be careful. The only thing standing between the grimoire and the people who wanted it so badly was me. And I'd like to avoid becoming anyone's punchbag or worse, thank you very much.

As I moved through the twisting labyrinth of Tumble Town, shadows seemed to stretch longer, and the air grew colder. I clutched my frontpack tighter, feeling the weight of the grimoire within. Maybe the chill was keeping folk inside because the streets were unusually quiet, save for the occasional distant barking of dogs or the squeaking of overhead signs or lamps on their heavy brackets. I refused to relax. My senses remained on high alert, every fibre of my being tuned to the slightest hint of danger.

Just as I was beginning to think I might make it to Humphrey's without incident, I reached Marlene Court. The lights in the art shop burned brightly, the window displays comforting in their normality and colourful familiarity when everything else in my world seemed to be constantly changing.

I heard the disturbance as soon as I stepped into Fire Beacon Lane. A caterwauling. Hesitantly I edged further into the lane, leaning forward, scanning the shadows. The closer I moved, the louder the ruckus became. Boys laughing. Not pleasantly. With malice. And they were a stone's throw away. In the burial place?

Boys can't hurt me, I told myself. This patently

wasn't true, but I was trying to instil myself with a confidence I didn't feel.

Something shrieked.

Not human.

Whatever it was, it was in pain.

I don't want to do this! I told myself before ignoring my own sage advice and rushing fully around the corner to confront the scene. "What's going on?" I yelled in my most adult and aggressive voice. "Get away! Get out of here!"

Whether it was the surprise of my sudden appearance or that I *did* actually appear threatening to them, the boys scattered, whooping and hollering —although not without throwing some foul-mouthed abuse my way once they were safely out of reach— and within seconds, I had the burial place to myself.

Almost to myself.

A pitiful crying drew my attention to a shadowy patch of ground between a tall Celtic cross on a crooked plinth and the rough stone wall belonging to the art shop. I inched closer, grimacing at the feel of mud squelching underfoot.

"Yow."

A cat?

I drew closer, gingerly crouching in order to see better.

"Yow."

"Hey, kitty." I used my soft voice. The voice of a woman who genuinely has no idea about how to approach or handle cats. The voice of a woman who had avoided them all her life. "Kitty kitty kitty—"

"Yowl."

It might have been my imagination, but the cat sounded annoyed by the baby talk.

"Alright." *Let's try a different approach.* "You're okay. Let me see you." No nonsense. "Come on, come here. Front and centre."

The cat poked its nose out of the shadow and into the muted light. "Yow."

It seemed calmer. I reached out tentatively. *Please don't scratch me.* The nose sniffed me.

"Yowl!"

Its miaow seemed altogether happier.

"Good ... cat! Out you come."

The cat dragged itself towards my hand and—much to my initial disgust—rubbed itself against me. Covered in mud, it had thin electrical wires tied to its back end and, I realised—notwithstanding that the thin wire could have caused a horrible amount of damage to the cat had it become more entangled—these wires were attached to a variety of implements the boys had collected locally. A couple of tin cans, a pair of pliers and a hammer, a bottle of water and a rusted tin sieve. I had no idea what the kids had intended, but I couldn't leave the poor creature like that. In the semi-darkness, I struggled with some of the knots, but eventually I was able to ease the trappings free of the cat's back end and cast them aside.

Satisfied, I sat back on my haunches and scratched the cat's ears. "There you are."

The cat steadily held my gaze. "Yowl."

There was something all too familiar about it. I scraped at the thick mud caking its face, revealing blue-grey fur. "Blue?"

"Yow."

"Oh, my life! Are you okay?" I hurried to clean him off.

"Yow." He sounded slightly pitiful. Either he was shaken—maybe even traumatised—or he was trying to elicit some sympathy.

I gently rubbed Blue's back, feeling the tremors of his body beneath my fingers. "It's okay, you're safe now," I murmured, trying to reassure him. Despite his bedraggled appearance, there was a spark in his eyes that reminded me what a little mischief-maker he was.

I cleaned him up as best I could, covering my robes in mud in the process. The thought of someone deliberately causing harm to such a helpless creature filled me with anger, but I needed to park that. My priority was to make sure Blue was alright.

Once I had removed most of the mud and debris, I picked him up. I'd never held him in my arms before and was surprised by how solid he felt. He relaxed a little in the warmth of my grasp as I cuddled him against the frontpack, his purring becoming a gentle hum. I decided I'd have to take him with me to Humphrey's house so that I could properly assess his condition.

Carrying Blue carefully, I stood up and made my way along the lane towards Humphrey's place. As we passed Murgatroyde's old dwelling—the windows and doors now properly boarded up—Blue raised his head.

"Yow!" he cried. "Yow."

Sensing he wanted some comfort, I stopped and tried my best to scritch him, although this was difficult given his position in front of the bag. "She's not there anymore," I reminded him.

"Yow." He sounded so mournful, my heart squeezed in sympathy. There was no way he'd been Murgatroyde's cat. He was young. She'd been dead for years. I couldn't get my head around his relationship to her.

"Let's go and get warm," I told him, and ambled the last few steps to Humphrey's front door.

Wearing a royal-blue pinafore apron—decorated somewhat incongruously with penguins—and clutching a wooden spoon, Humphrey opened the door with a flourish. He beamed at me and then dropped his gaze to Blue. "That's a cat."

"Well spotted."

"Is it who I think it is?"

"It is." I manoeuvred Blue about so that Humphrey could see him more clearly. "Humphrey meet Blue, Blue meet Humphrey."

Humphrey stepped back to allow me access to his hall. "He looks the worse for wear," he observed before looking me up and down. "As do you."

"I rescued him from some kids who were harassing him," I said, still angry about it. "Do you mind if I take him up to the bathroom and sponge him down? I don't know if cats like baths."

"They don't," said Humphrey knowingly. "But go ahead, we 'ave time. I'll dig out a couple of old towels."

"One will do," I said.

"I doubt that."

Humphrey was right. Even though I didn't directly turn the shower hose on Blue, he still squawked like a fish wife and fought me tooth and nail. By the time we'd finished, I was wetter than he was and had to dry myself off with the second towel.

The good news was that, in spite of a few cuts along Blue's back legs and a bald patch on his tail, he'd made it out of his encounter with the boys relatively unscathed. For my part, I had a feeling it would take days for my scratches to heal.

The scent of dinner—rich and beefy—tickled my tastebuds as we rejoined Humphrey downstairs.

"Good timing," he said when I popped my head around the kitchen door. "I've put a blanket on the floor for Blue. Make yourself at home."

I carefully deposited the still-damp Blue on a blanket by my chair before sitting at the diddly table. This could sit two at a push, because two sides were jammed into the corner. "Something smells delicious!"

"Oxtail casserole!" Humphrey announced and deposited a terracotta pot on the centre of the table before handing me a ladle. As I served myself, he sawed up some crusty bread, which he dropped into a basket and balanced—precariously—on the edge of the table. "Tell me about ya day," he said, joining me.

"I spent most of the day in the archives at the central library," I told him. I explained what I'd found and answered his questions about fountain pens and microfilms. Once we'd polished off the scrumptious supper, I showed him the photos I'd taken on my mobile.

"You hoping to speak to the policeman and this Barber man?" Humphrey asked, mopping up the rest of the casserole's gravy with the knob of the loaf.

"Yes. I popped in to see Ezra at the detective agency and he's going to try and find the detective for me, but whether I'll be able to track Mr K Barber down by myself, I don't know."

Humphrey pursed his lips, then purposefully turned to study Blue. Blue, apparently oblivious, was busy rewashing every part of his body. Evidently I hadn't done a good enough job. "Have you had a little chat with Blue yet?"

"What do you mean?" I asked, feeling a little daft. "Of course I've spoken to him—"

"Speaking *to* is not chatting *with*," Humphrey pointed out.

"Erm ..." I didn't know what to say to this.

Humphrey closed his eyes and shook his head. "I tell ya what," he said. "Why don't you go through to the parlour and get acquainted—"

Acquainted with the cat? "I already know who he is!"

"*Properly* acquainted, like. I'll join ya when I've cleaned up."

"I should be helping you wash up!" I said, pushing my chair back and starting to gather dishes.

"Absolutely not." Humphrey slapped at my hand. "You'll only break things and then I'll be forced to unfriend ya."

I wasn't entirely sure if he was being serious. "I—"

"Go!" He pointed at the door.

CHAPTER TWENTY-THREE

Perhaps Blue understood the assignment because as soon as I shepherded him into Humphrey's small parlour, he hopped up on the armchair, leaving the sofa to me. He sat upright, managing to look both elegant and distinguished even though his fur wasn't quite dry and he had a cut over his right eye that I hadn't noticed before.

"Oh no," I said, leaning in to examine it more closely. The wound was clean, from what I could see, and no longer bleeding. "I hope your fur grows back okay, or we'll have to call you Scarface."

"I've been called worse," said Blue.

I gasped and shot backwards, although there really wasn't enough room to do so. I collided with the coffee table and then the sofa. For a microcosm of time I hung in the air before collapsing onto the sofa with a squeak.

Blue blinked lazily at me, his eyes half closed in a manner that was both smug and nonchalant. "Did you seriously think I was just an ordinary cat?" he enquired, his voice rich with amusement.

"I-I didn't think you were, you know, a-a-a talking cat," I stammered, still trying to process the fact that the creature before me had spoken. "I didn't know that cats *could* talk."

"Well, now you do," Blue said, stretching his paws out before him. "There's more to this world than meets the eye, my dear."

"Whoa." I shook my head, attempting to clear the fog of disbelief. "Who ... What are you, then?"

Blue tilted his head, contemplating the question for a moment. "I am many things, but for now, let's just say I'm your ... guide."

"Guide? Guide to what?" I asked, curiosity getting the better of my initial shock.

"To the truth," he said simply, his tone suddenly serious. "There are secrets hidden in the grimoire, and it's about time you discovered them."

"I've been trying!" I reminded him.

"And to be fair to you, I think you've been doing a decent enough job. For an amateur."

"Thanks," I said. "I think." I frowned. "Amateur what?"

"Arcanologist."

"A who-y what?" The word rang a bell. Had Wizard Dodo referred to himself as such?

"Arcanologist. Someone who studies magick and the mystical within hidden or forbidden texts."

I did a double take. "Erm ... I think you have me mixed up with someone else. I issue permits. That's all I've ever done."

"It's not *all* you've ever done," Blue pointed out.

"If you're talking about university, that was a loooong time ago."

I'd never seen a cat roll its eyes before. Until now. "All of life's experiences build our skills."

"Mmm. But—"

"You may not have utilised them since you graduated but they'll still be there, hovering under your slightly dour exterior."

"Dour?" I repeated. "I'm not dour."

"When I first came across you, you were a sombre, introverted loner."

"I—"

"And now, see how you've metamorphosed! The past few days must have demonstrated that you're resilient and, ah ..." He blinked at me. "Quite brave, in fact."

I took a moment, then, "You think so?"

"I do."

"Gosh." I suppose I *had* been pushed out of my comfort zone. I took a moment to preen.

"And," Blue continued, "you have a good heart. I sensed that straight away. That's why I delivered the grimoire to you."

"So it *was* you! I knew it!"

"Of course." Blue smirked. "Who else?"

All of a sudden, words gushed from me like a torrent. "Where was it hidden? What's your relationship with Murgatroyde? Was she your—" I almost said owner, but that wouldn't do. I quickly corrected myself. "Were you her familiar?"

"Ah, Murgatroyde," Blue mused. "No. The first time I met her was when I led you next door."

I gawped at him, thoroughly confused. "But—"

"My acquaintance is with Pip, Murgatroyde's *only* familiar."

"Pip." I recalled the little brown mouse that had scampered around Murgatroyde's shoulders and underneath her hair on the day I met her in her kitchen. And then ... the mouse in the bedroom ... "But that couldn't have been the same one." I spoke the words out loud. Only half a thought, and yet Blue seemed to understand.

"*She* most certainly is the same one. She still lives next door. Returned there on Murgatroyde's sad passing. I met her when I sought shelter next door one particularly cold and stormy evening."

Putting aside that there was no earthly way a mouse could live that long, I struggled to believe a cat wouldn't chase and kill a mouse—

"That's something you're going to have to move past," Blue told me, his voice gentle but firm. "You can't simply limit your thinking to *earthly* ways. You must embrace the extra-natural and the supernatural. It's the only way you'll succeed."

"Succeed? As an arcanologist?"

"Exactly." He purred in satisfaction. "I think we're getting somewhere."

"Did Pip ask for your help?"

"With the grimoire? Kind of. She told me Murgatroyde's story. It seemed a terrible injustice to me. When Pip told me about the grimoire, I decided to borrow it—"

"You stole it—"

"Borrowed it, my dear." Blue narrowed his eyes. "I decided to borrow it and find someone who would be willing to help."

"You bludgeoned me into it," I complained and slumped back on the sofa, suddenly exhausted. "Why me?" I croaked.

Blue tilted his head, a thoughtful expression crossing his feline features. "Why does it matter? The universe has a way of choosing its champions. Perhaps it saw something in you that you have yet to see in yourself."

I frowned, feeling the weight of his words. "I just don't understand. I have no special talents, no extraordinary skills."

Blue's whiskers twitched with amusement. "Perhaps not in the conventional sense. But you possess curiosity, a thirst for knowledge and a resilient spirit. These are qualities that the arcane world values highly."

I took a deep breath, trying to process everything. "So, what now? What am I supposed to do?"

"Now," Blue said, his eyes gleaming with a mysterious light, "you begin your training. There is much to learn, much to discover. You will need all that resilience to find the other grimoires."

"Hang on!" I bolted upright. "Other grimoires? What other grimoires?"

"I believe they are listed in your grimoire—"

"But I haven't finished with Murgatroyde's yet. I still haven't cleared her name!"

Blue offered a beatific smile. "And you won't—not entirely—until the set is complete."

Panic rose in my chest. "Where are these others? How will I know where to find—"

"Patience. All will be revealed in time. They are hidden away from prying eyes and those who would do Murgatroyde wrong. Only the truly worthy can find them."

I opened and closed my mouth.

"*You* will find them." His yellow eyes sparkled. "With my help, of course."

"Of course," I mumbled faintly.

"And Pip's. She will answer more of your questions. You'd be wise to seek her counsel. She is many things—a teacher, a guide and, at times, a formidable adversary."

Great. I'd never wanted a pet, and now I had two.

"We will not be your pets," Blue told me sternly, either reading or sensing what was on my mind.

I gulped. "No, of course not." I took a deep breath and buried my face in my hands.

Blue broke into the turmoil of my thoughts. "You can say no. You don't have to do this."

I peeped at him through my fingers. *Tempting*, I thought. *Exceedingly tempting.*

"You can turn your back on it. Relinquish the first grimoire."

*The **first** grimoire. Hell's bells.*

"You can return to your old life. Scrabbling around for a modicum of joy."

"I won't find that at the Ministry of Witches," I muttered.

"And we don't want to lose you. You've already come such a long way." Blue's voice softened. "You have the potential to see beyond the surface. To be a great arcanologist. And now, the time has come for you to embrace that potential."

Stay or go? I wondered. Turn my back on Murgatroyde and her plight. And on Greta and Socrates. Didn't they deserve justice too? And what about the friends I'd made? Wootton, Ezra, Dodo, Humphrey!

Not to mention Blue.

I couldn't give up yet. I needed to see it through. "I'll probably lose my job," I said.

Blue shrugged. "Probably."

I sighed. "Where do we start?"

Blue's eyes sparkled with a mix of mischief and wisdom. "We start with what's right in front of us. Now. Are you ready to see the unseen?"

Trepidation mixed with anticipation. I sensed this was the beginning of something extraordinary. Rubbing my stomach, wishing I hadn't eaten quite so much of Humphrey's excellent casserole, I nodded.

"Let's do it."

CHAPTER TWENTY-FOUR

"Where are we going?" I hissed.

After letting Humphrey know I was popping out—Humphrey didn't bat an eyelid when Blue spoke to him!—Blue had led me to the front door.

"Let me get my robes," I'd said, remembering how cold it was out there this evening, but Blue had tsk-tsked impatiently.

"There's no need. We're not going far."

By that I'd thought he meant we were slipping inside Murgatroyde's dwelling, maybe so I could be formally introduced to Pip, but apparently not. Blue swaggered past the boarded-up door, his tail in the air.

I trotted behind him, already regretting the

absence of my robes. Filthy they might be, but at least they'd have kept me warm and dry.

"Just a little further," Blue sang.

True to his word, we stopped outside number 6 Fire Beacon Lane. This tiny dwelling, probably a two-up and two-down, had a sagging roof, a tall chimney and early-Georgian-style, narrow sash windows. From where I stood, the place appeared derelict.

"Are we going in there?" I whispered.

"You want to speak to Mr Barber, don't you?"

The *dead* Mr Barber? "I do as it happens. Are we going to break in?"

Blue gave me a sly smile, his whiskers twitching with mischievous delight. "Break in? No, no. I have a key."

With a swift flick of his paw, a small, tarnished key appeared, glinting in the moonlight. He hopped up to the door, inserting the key into the old lock. The mechanism creaked and groaned in protest but finally yielded with a grating click. The door swung open, revealing a dark, musty interior.

"After you." Blue gestured grandly, sweeping his tail in an exaggerated bow.

I hesitated for a moment, peering into the shadowy entrance. The air inside was stale, heavy with the scent of mildew and forgotten memories. Summoning my courage—remembering that I'd literally chosen this new life only five minutes before—I stepped over the threshold, my footsteps echoing on the worn wooden floor.

Blue padded silently beside me, his eyes gleaming with some secret knowledge. The narrow hallway led us into the house, past the front room filled with cobwebs and dust-covered furniture. It was as if time had stood still within these walls, preserving the remnants of a life long since abandoned.

At the end of the hall, we came to a door slightly ajar. From behind it, a faint, otherworldly glow emanated, casting eerie shadows on the walls. I turned to Blue, seeking reassurance, but he merely nodded towards the door, urging me forward. "Go on."

With a deep breath, I pushed the door open and stepped into the room. The sight before me took my breath away. The room was bathed in an ethereal light, and in the centre, the spectral figure of Mr Barber, his translucent form flickering like a candle flame, sat in a rocking chair, a crocheted blanket over his spindly knees.

Blue sat on his haunches, his tail curled around

his paws, and watched with an air of satisfaction as I approached Mr Barber. I shivered, but this was what I'd wanted, wasn't it? A chance to speak with the dead and uncover the secrets that had drawn me into this eerie adventure.

"Who's there?"

I glanced at Blue.

He nodded encouragement, but still I hesitated. It was one thing talking to Ezra, but Mr Barber was sitting here, rocking gently away and minding his own eternal business.

Blue made a hissing noise and marched up to Mr Barber, rubbing himself against the old man's legs. I'd bet any money you like that if I tried to do that, I wouldn't have been able to feel a thing, but here was Blue interacting with a ghost as though the metaphysical had become physical.

"Ah, Blue." Mr Barber chuckled. "Where have you been?"

"Business, Ken! You know how it is."

"You are the busiest, tricksiest cat I know!" Mr Barber grinned, reaching down to tickle him. "Always paws deep in some plot or other." He stared in my direction, but not quite at me. "Who do you have with you?"

"This is Zilla," Blue told him. "She'd like to ask you some questions."

"Would she indeed?"

I cleared my throat. "Yes, hello. I'm Zilla Chaplin. I'm sorry to disturb you," I began.

"A *young* woman?" Mr Barber sounded surprised. "Don't be sorry. I don't mind answering questions. I don't have anything else to do after all, but I do have a long time in which to do nothing."

"She apologises constantly," Blue told him, hopping onto the old man's thigh. "It can get a tad wearisome."

"I'm sorry about that," I said.

"I rest my case." Blue curled up on top of the blanket on the old man's lap. I sensed that this wasn't the first time he'd done so.

"Good evening to you, Zilla. Ignore Blue. He can be obstreperous at times. It's nice for me to have visitors. Take a pew," Mr Barber suggested.

I looked around the cluttered kitchen with its rusting pots and pans and congealed grease. I wasn't keen, but I opted for a rickety old stool and perched, rather awkwardly, a few feet from Mr Barber so I could hear and be heard.

But not seen as it turned out.

"I'm blind," Mr Barber said when I'd settled

myself. "So there won't be any point in showing me anything."

That gave me pause. Had he been blind in 1958?

He answered my question for me. "I haven't always been blind. I had some loss of vision the last few years of my life but only lost my sight completely a few months before I passed away."

"I'm sorry," I said and could have kicked myself. *Will you shut up!* To cover my discomfort, I hurried on. "I'd like to ask you some questions about events at the burial place—"

I didn't need to go any further.

"You're here about the children," Mr Barber said.

"I am."

"I haven't spoken about them for a long while. People were interested at the time, but like all these things, time passes, people forget."

"Murgatroyde Plunge wouldn't have forgotten," I said.

"No." Mr Barber dipped his head. "Poor Murgatroyde."

"You knew her?"

Mr Barber took a moment. Blue purred into the silence as though encouraging the old fella to share his memories. When he finally did, I must admit I was gobsmacked, but in the nicest possible way.

"Intimately," he told me. "We were lovers for a while."

"I see."

"I suppose I should backtrack a little. I knew her when we were both terribly young. We didn't go to the same schools but, around this area of Cheapside, everyone knew everyone and all the kids used to run wild through the streets together." He smiled at the memory. "Ah. I thought she was so pretty with her wild hair and her big smile. Of course, she outgrew hanging around with silly little boys soon enough, most of the girls did. Besides, she was studious, after a fashion. Went off to the Witches College of Art, whereas I studied physics. I specialised in portal magick."

"Wow," I said, impressed.

"It's not half as interesting as it sounds." Mr Barber sniffed. "It's just maths and a wand."

I doubted that, but I let him continue.

"I met Murgatroyde again when working on a portal at Hecate Primary School. She was doing some teaching there and we chatted, went on a date and took it from there. She bought the dwelling down the lane, partly to be closer to me, I think, although she never said so." He grinned. "She liked it because it had the shop on the front.

She wanted to open her own gallery one day. Display her art."

"Awww." The thought of her doing that punched me in the gut. All the dreams she'd had.

"We never formalised any sort of relationship. She wasn't interested. Liked to play it fast and a bit loose."

I nodded.

"A social butterfly," he said, then smiled. "What about you? Are you a social butterfly?"

Pfft! "No. I'm more of a social spider," I told him.

"Ah!" He perked up at this. "You like to ensnare your prey?"

"No." I narrowed my eyes. "I was thinking more of hiding in dark corners out of people's way."

"That explains why you're single," Blue said.

"And staying that way," I replied. "Best-case scenario? I'm the spider that isn't invited to the party in the first place."

Mr Barber tittered. "When I was younger I'd have changed your mind. Life is for living."

Over the last few days, I can honestly say that I was beginning to feel that way. Nevertheless, I steered our conversation back on course.

"Can you remember what happened that night?" I asked. "The night the children were killed?"

Mr Barber took a minute before speaking slowly. "You know, sometimes ... in dreams ... I think I can remember ... but then afterwards ... everything has become so clouded. By age. By what I've read in the newspapers. By conversations I've had with others. There's no clarity."

My heart sank. This wasn't what I wanted to hear.

"So, I can tell you what I think I remember, but you're better off taking it with a grain of salt."

"I understand."

He licked his lips. Perhaps, on whatever plane he inhabited, he was thirsty. "Kids were always playing out there in the burial place, and back then, if I recall correctly, it had become a real problem."

He tickled Blue's ears.

"They would sneak in there at night, daring each other to stay the longest," Mr Barber continued. "To remain there until the witching hour. It was a game of courage, or maybe just foolishness, but it was their playground. It annoyed me—so much at times that I even made a complaint to the parish, but what could they do? What would they do? One afternoon, late afternoon, there was a terrible storm. The wind howled like a beast and the rain came down in sheets. I remember walking home from work and hurrying to get inside, grateful for the warmth of the fire. It had eased off by about seven, I think, and I do recall hearing shouting and screams, but ..." He sighed. "I didn't think anything of it."

He paused, his gaze distant as if peering into the past. "The next morning, they found the little boy. The authorities were everywhere, but nobody knew what had happened. They searched high and low for the girl but found no trace. It was as if the storm itself had stolen her away."

The room fell silent, the weight of his words hanging in the air. I could feel the chill of the memory creeping into the present, wrapping around us like a fog.

And then, Mr Barber sighed. "You must understand, the events of that night ... they haunt me. But the details, they slip away like sand through my fingers. I wish I could give you more."

"Mmm." I nodded, absorbing the fragments he'd offered, even as my mind raced. "Murgatroyde was well-acquainted with the burial place," I confirmed. "I mean, she had to walk past it every day, and if she visited you, she couldn't miss it."

"Obviously."

"And people around here would have known her. Not just you."

"Indeed."

"So—to me—it makes no sense for her to kill the children on her front doorstep."

"I always thought that," Mr Barber acknowledged. "The police didn't agree."

"And ..." I grasped at the absurdity of it all. "Why wouldn't she have knocked on your door? If it was an accident, you would have helped her."

"Of course. We would have taken the boy to a hospital. But the police didn't like that idea because the girl was missing."

I exhaled noisily. "So much of this depends on Greta, doesn't it?"

"The ground was sodden out there. The police claimed there were drag marks that proved that either Greta's body had been removed, or she had been dragged alive and spirited away somewhere else, but I fail to see how Murgatroyde could have done that. She was only slight herself. How far could she have carried her?"

"The newspapers said there were symbols carved in the earth."

"Nonsense. Who would have been able to see them? The ground had been completely churned up."

"Hmmm. And you didn't see Murgatroyde that night at all?"

"I never saw her again," Mr Barber replied, and now he sounded sorrowful. "I wasn't allowed to see her on remand, and she wrote to me after the trial telling me to forget about her. She couldn't face seeing anyone she knew. I did reply, and I wrote several times over the years, but my letters were always returned to me."

"Oh." I thought my heart would break.

We sat in silence for a while. Mr Barber sniffed a few times and swiped at his face. Blue lay very still in his lap.

Finally, I stirred. My backside was hurting and anyway, I ought to get back to Humphrey's. "Thank you," I said softly, sensing that Mr Barber had given all he could.

But he hadn't finished. "You know, I've hardly mentioned this to anyone before, but I do know of someone who saw Murgatroyde that night."

"Who?" I asked, sitting upright.

"Lizzie-Free Pillinger."

I shook my head. The name meant nothing to me.

My silence must have indicated my ignorance because Mr Barber continued. "She owned

Pillinger's Art Products and Craft Store at the time. I believed the police interviewed her on the day the boy was found, but I'm not sure how forthcoming Lizzie-Free may have been."

"How come?"

"She and Murgatroyde were well-acquainted—even friends, dare I say it—because Murgatroyde spent an absolute fortune in there. From time to time Murgatroyde would teach classes for groups of three or four of Lizzie-Free's customers, or she'd help Lizzie-Free out with the shop if her son wasn't there."

I nodded, wondering what was coming. "Uh-huh."

"Lizzie-Free, she must have been in her late sixties, early seventies and had become somewhat frail. After Murgatroyde's arrest I bumped into her in the street and we—like everyone—chatted about what had happened. She couldn't understand Murgatroyde's arrest. She claimed that Murgatroyde had visited the shop late that afternoon and they'd spent a good few hours together. Murgatroyde was helping her reorganise her stockroom. That's what she told me. They ate supper together, and then Murgatroyde went home sometime after nine."

"And Lizzie-Free didn't mention this to the police?"

"Oh, she did. The police said Murgatroyde could have committed the murders before or after her time in the shop—"

"What nonsense!" I exclaimed in annoyance. "I swear the police were grasping at straws. It's almost ... it's almost— oh my goodness." It hadn't occurred to me before. "Do you think they were trying to frame Murgatroyde for the murders?"

"It seems possible, doesn't it?" Mr Barber agreed. "I wouldn't have thought it of the detective in charge. He seemed like a decent type, but who knows?"

"Why wasn't Lizzie-Free called to give evidence at the trial?" I asked.

"Sadly she passed away beforehand. She hadn't been well for a while." He rocked gently in his chair. "I always felt that after the events of that night, the neighbourhood changed. It was never the same."

"Do you think I should try to speak to Lizzie-Free?" I asked.

"You could try, but she'll only confirm what I've said."

I nodded and sighed. "Yes."

Speaking to DS Larch would probably be a better use of my time. A meeting with the detective seemed essential if I was to discover the true intentions of his investigation. I wondered whether Ezra had managed to find anything out yet.

I gathered my thoughts and rose from my seat, thanking Mr Barber. Blue finally made a move, stretching and scratching himself before bumping Mr Barber's nose with his own and leaping gracefully from his perch.

"Pop around any time you like," Mr Barber said, and I promised I would.

CHAPTER TWENTY-FIVE

"May I help you?"

A woman with multicoloured hair peered across at me as I entered the detective agency the following afternoon.

She was alone in the office, apart from Ezra. Wizard Dodo was nowhere to be seen.

"I, erm ..." I glanced over at Ezra's desk. He'd assumed his usual position, feet up on the desk, trilby over his face, sudoku book with the broken spine lying open in front of him.

"Oh, hey, Zilla!" Wootton burst into the office from a back room clutching a handful of paper. "How are you doing?"

"Great," I said automatically, like we Brits always do.

"Zilla's here to see Ezra," Wootton told the colourful woman, handing her the sheaf of papers.

"Ah." She nodded.

Wootton made the introductions. "Zilla, this is Elise. Boss, this is Zilla."

So this was Elise. To match her wonderful hair, she'd been blessed with flawless skin and looked as fit as a flea. Though at least ten years older than me, I felt slightly envious of her amazing glow.

"Pleased to meet you." Elise held out her hand and I shook it. Her hands were warm, mine were icy. I'd forgotten my gloves. "Brrr!" she said and laughed. "You're one of Ezra's clients?"

Clients? Oh. Oops. Were they going to charge me for services rendered?

Wootton came to my rescue. "Don't worry, Elise," he said. "It's all taken care of."

Was it? I didn't quite know where to put myself. But Elise took what Wootton said at face value. She pulled a face and winked at me. "As you can see, there's a queue for his services. You may have to wait a while." With that, she laughed and grabbed her bag. "Don't mind me. I've got to dash."

Wootton indicated that I could go over. As soon as I approached Ezra's desk, the detective removed his hat and sat up. "Zilla! I was hoping you'd show up. I have news."

I settled myself in the chair opposite. "Me too."

"You do?"

"You go first," I said, keen to learn what he'd discovered.

"I called in a few favours and found out that DS Larch hangs out in a tavern near the river."

"So we can go and see him?" I asked.

"There are a few complications."

Of course there are, I thought.

"Namely, that the tavern has been condemned and is officially standing empty."

"Surely that just makes our job easier?" I suggested, unsure what he meant by 'officially'.

"You'd think so, wouldn't you?" Ezra replied. "The thing is, my sources tell me the place still operates and has its regulars. That means he's not alone. I don't have a clue what's gone on with Bill or why, but he seems to have surrounded himself with a bunch of criminals."

"Okay." I was liking the sound of this much less.

"With that in mind, I've decided that if we're going to see him, then we'll need some protection."

I glanced over at Wootton, who was earwigging on our conversation.

"Hey, don't look at me," he said, genuinely horrified. "I'm no heavyweight."

"I'm not thinking we need heavyweights," Ezra said, probably in response to the look on my face. "Only that there is strength in numbers."

"So you're taking an army?" Wootton joked.

"No. Better than that, even." Ezra settled back in his chair, a serious look on his face. "I had Elise call in Minsk."

Wootton whistled. "Big guns indeed!"

This sounded reassuring but also slightly terrifying. The name Minsk conjured up images of a hefty chap around seven feet tall, with a great fluffy ushanka hat crowning his head and covering his ears and carrying a Kalashnikov.

"Now tell me your news," Ezra said, and I took him through the conversation I'd had the previous evening with Mr Barber.

Ezra had pulled his tatty notebook and stubby pencil from his pocket to sketch out a few notes. "We may need to corroborate his story about Murgatroyde's whereabouts at the time of the children's disappearance sometime in the future, but I agree that it's beginning to look doubtful she did it."

I felt a jolt of happy relief. *Finally*! Finally,

someone else believed Murgatroyde. At least potentially. It was a big step.

"And, as you say, there's a reason to suspect that the initial investigation was flawed." Ezra nodded in satisfaction. "Another reason to have Minsk with us this evening."

"Who is this mysterious Minsk?" I asked.

"Dark Squad," said Wootton.

"Dark Squad?" I'd never heard of them.

"They're a special branch of the Ministry of Witches Police Department. They tend to deal with darker supernatural crimes, criminals and criminal gangs. They have a special knack for finding people who don't want to be found. You don't mess with them."

"Our Elise has some special links with them," Wootton said. "For better or worse."

"I see," I said, although I wasn't sure I did. A sudden thought occurred to me though. "Do you think they'd know anything about Greta?"

Ezra pondered on this. "You're thinking she wasn't killed with Socrates."

"I know some of the evidence suggests she was, but I can't understand how her body was never found—"

"Probably in the Thames," said Wootton.

Ezra rolled his eyes. "That's imaginative, Wootton."

"There's been no trace of her since that night and I'm morbidly curious, I suppose." I shrugged.

"Maybe she did get away," Wootton agreed. "Maybe she's still alive. You should put her photo in one of those AI apps."

Puzzled, I frowned at him. "Pardon?"

"You know, artificial intelligence? There are apps that can age photos. You'd be able to see what she might look like now."

I smiled. "Is there genuinely such a thing?"

"Several. Some are better than others. Do you have a photo?"

"On my phone."

"Forward it to me," he said.

I fiddled with my phone and finally managed to send the image across to him. "Leave it with me," he said. "I'll run it through a couple of apps and send the best versions back to you."

"That'll be interesting!" I enthused. "Thanks!"

"Mod cons, eh?" Ezra sniffed. "In my day we used police artists—"

"In your day, dinosaurs still roamed the earth," Wootton taunted and I chuckled quietly.

"So, what's the plan?" I asked Ezra.

"Meet me at Marlene Court at midnight," Ezra said. "Bring a wand if you have one."

I grimaced. "A wand? I haven't used a wand for years."

Ezra shrugged. "Times change. But trust me, you'll need it tonight."

Wootton nodded solemnly. "Ezra's right. Better to be safe than sorry."

I sighed, feeling apprehensive. "Alright, I'll dig it out. Midnight it is."

CHAPTER TWENTY-SIX

I stood under a street lamp and shivered. The night had turned cold. There'd be a frost in the morning, for sure. Every time I breathed out I exhaled a cloud. No matter how old I become, I'm always going to enjoy doing that.

The lights in the art shop were on—which I'd expect, even at this hour—but I couldn't see any customers. *How do they make enough money to stay open?* I wondered before tilting my head to stare at the windows on the upper storey.

"Do you think Lizzie-Free is up there?"

Ezra, wearing his long mackintosh and trilby and looking every inch the detective, apparated beside me, making me jump. "You could have given me some notice!" I hissed, palpating my heart.

Ezra pointed a finger into the air next to his ear, inviting me to listen. The clock on the Ministry of Witches dome marked the hour with its deep tintinnabulous bongs. "I said midnight," he reminded me.

Smarty pants.

"Are we all here?" he asked, and I glanced around, expecting hordes. I couldn't see anyone else, let alone a burly police officer in a huge fur hat. I'd considered asking Humphrey to come along with me, but this wasn't his fight. I hadn't been able to locate Blue either, although I had an inkling he'd be hiding out somewhere warm.

Good for him.

"All present and correct," said a small female voice from the shadows.

I squinted down the empty lane to my right. At first I couldn't see anything, but then a white rabbit with chocolate eyes hopped into view.

"Good to see you, Minsk," said Ezra. "This is Zilla. Zilla, this is Minsk."

I'm sure my mouth must have dropped open. Minsk wasn't what I'd been expecting at all. I mean ... a rabbit?

"Good to meet you," said Minsk, thankfully paying no attention to my overt rudeness. "It sounds like an interesting case you're involved with."

I recovered myself. "I would love to be able to prove Murgatroyde Plunge was innocent, but at the moment it all depends on the say-so of ghosts."

"I'm always happy to work with ghost witness testimony," Minsk said. "Sometimes it's the best kind."

"Let's get going," Ezra said. "I don't want any rogue Shadow People alerting DS Larch to our approach."

"After you," said Minsk, and I fell in behind Ezra as he took the right-hand lane towards the river. I had a vague recollection of this route from being chased down here the other night. Narrow and twisty, I sensed that every step deeper into Tumble Town took us past older neighbourhoods, and the deeper we went, the darker the residents.

Even the smells spoke of poverty and decay. Alternately acrid or acidic, rotting wood, rust and oil. Bonfires, chimneys, animals. Darker aromas ... I closed my mind to them.

As we pressed on, the dim light of the street-lamps cast elongated shadows, dancing eerily against crumbling brick walls and broken windows. The silence was punctuated only by the occasional scuttling of rodents, the whispers of unseen Shadow People and the distant clatter of a cart. I frequently found myself glancing back at Minsk, half expecting her to vanish into the shadows like some conjured figment of my imagination.

Ezra moved with a determined stride—although in effect, he was floating—his figure a reassuring silhouette against the encroaching gloom. I could sense his urgency as the lane twisted and turned, leading us past shuttered windows and doors that looked like they hadn't been opened in years. Occasionally, a flicker of movement through heavy net curtains hinted at the lives that persisted in this forgotten part of town. The further we went, the more oppressive the atmosphere became, as if the very air was thick with the whispers of the past.

When we finally reached the riverbank, the murky waters shrouded in mist lapped quietly against the wooden stilts of the gangways. Ezra paused, turning to us with a grave expression. "This is where we need to be," he said, his voice barely more than a murmur.

With a nod, Minsk and I followed him towards an old, rickety bridge that stretched across a river inlet. The wood creaked ominously under our weight, but we pressed on, driven by the promise of uncovering the secrets that had long been buried in Tumble Town.

Over the bridge and a swift left and right, then Ezra stopped and pointed. Breathlessly coming alongside him, I regarded the short street. A narrow cul-de-sac, there were perhaps a dozen tiny terraced houses to my right—some in better condition than others—and five on the left, crooked and broken like a pauper's teeth. The tavern, a ramshackle, sagging, sorry excuse for a building—probably Georgian or older—sat between two vacant lots. There'd been dwellings on either side, but they'd long gone.

"What's your thinking?" Minsk asked Ezra.

"They're going to know we're here," Ezra said. "There's not going to be any element of surprise."

Isn't there? my internal voice squeaked. *Shouldn't there be?*

"Might as well knock, then," Minsk decided. "All friendly, like."

Ezra nodded and headed for the tavern.

"Erm ..." I swallowed. "Are they going to be friendly in return?"

"It's not something you can always count on," Minsk said.

"But you do have your wand, don't you?" Ezra asked without looking back.

I laughed, more in despair than amusement, and reached into my pocket for my short Ministry of Witches wand before hurrying after the others.

Although the tavern couldn't have been in operation for many a year, its sign swung freely above our heads, creating a grating sound designed to put every last nerve on edge. I blinked up at it. The Hanging Man.

Oh, isn't that just dandy? I thought. *Is it too late to turn around?*

Ezra had other ideas. He was already knocking on the front door. As I came to stand next to him, I distinctly heard the sound of music and people chatting. Maybe the tavern was operational after all?

After a few seconds, a tiny iron slat in the door was pulled back and a pair of eyes—or rather one live eye and one dead eye—glared out at us. "Ooo goes there?" a voice rasped.

Ezra held up empty hands. "DS Ezra Izax and my colleagues."

The slat shot closed.

"Iz the fuzz," the voice inside the pub announced.

The music stopped. A deadly hush fell ... Silence. Apart from the ominous groan of The Hanging Man sign.

But then the door creaked open, revealing a dimly lit interior filled with the scent of stale ale and smoke. The patrons within—mostly men, but there were a few women, heavily made up—turned their heads in unison, their eyes narrowing as they scrutinised us newcomers. I realised there was a mixture of physical people and ghosts, as though this were a place where both sides of the veil could raise a glass together for old times' sake.

Ezra stepped in boldly, his shoulders squared—it was alright for him, he was already dead—while Minsk and I, all flesh and blood, followed with more caution. "We're looking for someone," Ezra declared, his voice carrying through the room. "We have reason to believe we'll find him here."

The barman, a skinny, balding fellow with braces and a stained shirt and apron, set a glass down on the counter, hard enough to make me jump.

At this, a large, burly man with a scar running down his cheek stood up from his seat near the fireplace. "And what gives you reason to assume he's here?" he growled, his tone as menacing as his appearance.

Minsk hopped forward. "We have ... information to that effect," she said, her voice steady. Fearless.

The burly man growled. "What makes you think we'll hand him over?"

"We were hoping for a friendly conversation." Minsk's gaze swept the room, resting now and again on individuals. "We're only interested in one person. If we get what we want, we'll leave here in peace."

The tension in the room was palpable. I could feel the weight of a dozen suspicious gazes upon us, and my grip tightened on my wand. Nobody else moved.

The burly man snarled. "You should know better than to come 'ere."

"We definitely wouldn't if we didn't have to," Ezra told him.

Burly Man looked from Ezra to Minsk to me and back to Ezra. "A ghost, a rabbit and a kid? You're either brave or stupid."

I'm not a kid! I bristled but I wasn't about to speak up. This was proper grown-up business, and even at twenty-eight, I was feeling out of my depth.

"Probably a bit of both," Ezra said. "We're looking for DS Bill Larch."

Despite nobody seeming to move an inch, I could feel a ripple of consternation spread outwards from the bar.

"Why would a copper hang out here?" Burly Man asked.

"I can only imagine he has friends in low places," said Ezra.

The silence that followed almost stopped my heart. It was like a lull before a hand grenade exploded. I don't believe anyone actually breathed for some time until Burly Man guffawed—and when he did, everyone else joined in. Even the sour-faced barman. People resumed chattering and drinking, with half an eye on proceedings.

Apart from Burly Man, that is. He studied Ezra with an intense look in his eyes. "And what, hyper-fetick-ly speaking, if we don't serve this bloke up to you?"

Before Ezra could respond, Minsk hopped forward to the man's feet and tilted her head up to stare him straight in the eye. "Then—and this is *hypothetically* speaking too—we'd have to raid the premises, cart you all for questioning—and that would mean mugshots and fingerprinting too—and then we'd bulldoze the pub and put an end to your smuggling ring, *Mr Cappy*."

Burly Man jolted.

The whole tavern fell silent again.

"It *is* Mr Cappy, isn't it?" Minsk asked politely.

"Bernard 'the pirate' Cappy? Skipper of the *Light-Fingered*, currently berthed at Deadman's Wharf?"

Burly Man glowered at Minsk, his jaw set hard.

"You've got the wrong guy," Cappy said through gritted teeth, though the sweat beading on his forehead told an entirely different story.

Minsk didn't waver. "Oh, I don't think so. You see, we've been following your little escapades for months now. The *Light-Fingered* isn't as sneaky on the water as you'd like to believe."

A murmur spread through the tavern as the patrons exchanged worried glances. Cappy's eyes flicked around the room, noting the rising tension.

"How are you doing, Rita?" Minsk called to a woman with hair like a powder puff, the rouge on her cheeks as red as her lipstick. "Your old man enjoying his stretch at Witchwood Scrubbs?"

The woman cursed Minsk with language so blue, I could feel my cheeks flush.

Minsk only laughed and raised her voice so that everyone could hear her. "Listen up, friends! I suggest everyone either stays clear of us or assists us in our endeavours. There is no third way. Not for you. Not for this tavern. Not today."

Ezra took a step forward, his presence

commanding attention. "Now, Mr Cappy, we can do this the easy way or the hard way. Your choice."

Cappy's shoulders slumped ever so slightly, a sign of resignation. "Alright," he said, a defeated tone creeping into his voice. "The back room. Through the door at the rear. In the cellar."

Ezra's smile was predatory. "That was easy, wasn't it?"

After a moment's hesitation, Cappy nodded. Slowly but surely, the tension in the room dissipated, the other patrons gradually returning to their drinks and conversations, the threat of violence averted—for now.

Minsk shot a quick look at Ezra, who nodded almost imperceptibly. "Let's go," she said.

CHAPTER TWENTY-SEVEN

The back room of The Hanging Man was not a place any decent witch or wizard would want to hang out.

As I pushed through saloon-style doors—Ezra glided through them, Minsk slipped under them—my eyes began to sting immediately. The air was thick with cigarette and cigar smoke. To my left was the bar that wrapped itself around the centre of the building, so that the same barman was working both areas. Several men were leaning against the bar, staring into the bottom of their glasses. At the far end of the building—which wasn't actually that far—was a pool table with several men and women engrossed in a match. Between these two points was a round table with a group of men absorbed in a game of poker.

In the shadows, card players muttered to each other, the clinking of poker chips punctuating their hushed conversation. Minsk and Ezra moved with purpose, weaving through the haze and the flickering light of old oil lamps that cast long, wavering shadows across the room.

Ezra's form seemed to glow faintly, an ethereal contrast to the dingy surroundings. At the poker table, the men barely glanced up, their attention ensnared by the game and the prospect of winning—or losing—small fortunes.

As we approached the far end of the room, a figure detached itself from the darkness, stepping into a sliver of light. It was a tall man, his face partially obscured by a wide-brimmed hat. He didn't move, merely studied us with quiet menace.

Ezra inclined his head slightly, acknowledging the man's presence. "We're here for business. Let's keep this professional."

The man's eyes flicked to Minsk, to me, then back to Ezra. "Professional, huh?" He smirked, revealing a row of rotting teeth. "We'll see about that."

Ignoring the man's taunt, Ezra continued to the

back of the room where a heavy wooden door stood, reinforced with iron bands. Ezra pressed his hand to the door, and for a moment, his form seemed to shimmer more brightly. Then the door creaked open, revealing a narrow staircase descending into darkness.

Without hesitation, Ezra and Minsk descended, so I hurried after them.

"Hey!" the man with bad teeth shouted, but he didn't come after us.

The door swung shut behind me. The wooden steps were barely lit, but Ezra had his wand out and the light saved me from missing a step. The atmosphere below was colder, damper, and the sound of dripping water echoed through the narrow stairwell. The soft pad of Minsk's paws was almost silent, while Ezra's ghostly form made no noise at all. Every step I took, however, seemed scarily loud.

We reached another door, this one scraped and dull with age. Ezra pushed it open, revealing a small room cluttered with crates and barrels. At a rickety table sat a lone man—another ghost—wearing a trilby and smoking a pipe, playing solitaire with a tatty pack of cards.

He barely acknowledged us, simply dealt another card.

"DS Larch?" Ezra asked.

"Retired," said the man, laying down a two of spades.

"We'd like to ask you some questions."

The man—Larch—sighed and finally looked up, his gaze drifting over us one by one. "Dead copper, Dark Squad, civil servant. What do you want?"

I blinked. Had I worked at the Ministry of Witches so long I even looked like a civil servant? Holy moly. I'd be shaving my hair off, dying it pink and having half a dozen face piercings first thing tomorrow.

"We'd like some information about a case you worked on," Ezra said.

Larch frowned. "You're reopening a case?"

"Potentially," Minsk said in her sing-song voice. I admired the way she always sounded like she was enjoying herself.

"Socrates and Greta Mayflower," Ezra said without any more preamble.

Larch didn't flinch. "That case was solved. The murderer went down for a long stretch." He returned to his game of solitaire.

I couldn't let this pass. "Murgatroyde Plunge did not murder those children!"

"Who's the fan girl?" Larch asked Ezra, not bothering to look at me.

Before either Minsk or Ezra could stop me, I charged forward and slapped his table so hard it hurt my palm. I expected the cards to jump out of position, but they were ghost cards and remained neatly in their columns. "Don't patronise me!"

"Zilla—" Ezra began.

I waved him away. "I'm not a fan girl," I told Larch. "I'm trying to correct a terrible injustice—"

"A jury of her peers found her guilty," Larch reminded me.

"And you helped them do that," I said. "You buried witness testimony that could have exonerated her."

Larch cast a side-eye at Minsk. She grinned at him. You've never seen a rabid rabbit until you've seen the knowing smile on a Dark Squad rabbit.

"You mean that old biddy at the shop?" Larch mocked. "An unreliable witness."

"We can visit Lizzie-Free if we need to," Minsk told him. "And Murgatroyde Plunge's lover."

Larch shook his head. "Barber? No-one would have believed him—he was too close to Plunge. He was lying to save her skin."

Minsk tilted her head lazily. "If you insist on

remaining so unforthcoming, DS Larch, my supervisor has given me permission to take a closer look at all your cases and all your ... *associates*."

For the first time, I saw something in Larch's eye that might have been apprehension. He glanced around, staring into the shadows as though he expected to find someone there.

"You don't want to mess with Superintendent Culpeper," Minsk continued. "I mean, *there's* a man you don't want to cross whether you're dead or alive. He could make things extremely uncomfortable for you."

Larch shifted in his seat. "Culpeper, eh?"

"It doesn't have to go that far," I said, trying to appeal to his better nature. "I know you know that Murgatroyde was innocent. Please—"

I got no further. Before I could react, Larch jumped out of his seat and icy fingers wrapped themselves around my neck. I'd never been touched by a ghost before, and I squealed in surprise. Something pointed pressed against my temple, and I was jerked around to face Minsk and Ezra.

I gasped.

"Stay still," Minsk told me, her voice carefully controlled.

"Ha-a-a-ah!" I didn't have much choice.

"Come on, Larch. Let her be," Ezra said, sounding almost jovial. "Like you said, she's only a civil servant. She's harmless."

"Totally harmless," I agreed.

"There's too much at stake," Larch hissed. "I can't let you take me in."

Ezra gestured at the table, the solitaire cards still laid out. "What sort of an afterlife is this though?"

"It's better than the alternative."

Ezra shook his head. "What are you doing here? Are you in hiding? Or is someone else hiding you away to protect themselves?"

"Shhhh!" Larch screeched through gritted teeth before adding, "I'd rather stay here than languish in some distant prison colony somewhere, or—"

"Or?" Ezra pressed, but Larch only dug his fingers tighter into my neck and scowled.

"Ach!" I squawked.

"Or ... are you up to your neck in something you shouldn't be? Police corruption? Maybe you were taking backhanders from some of the people you should have been arresting—"

"Shut up!" Larch spat, again glancing furtively towards the back end of the cellar where the shadows were densest.

"A bit of both, I'm guessing," said Minsk, her nose twitching.

"You don't know what you're saying," Larch whispered.

"Or who we'll upset?" Ezra asked, his eyes narrowing. "Who are you frightened of, Bill?"

"No-one!"

"You needn't worry about us," Minsk added. "You know the Dark Squad always get their foe!"

"No," said Larch, pinching me so tightly my eyes began to water. As I blinked tears away, I realised two figures had emerged from the darkness. They were moving quickly and, like a bolt of lightning, threw themselves towards us.

"Watch out!" I managed to shriek, and then everything happened far too quickly for me to process. Ezra turned, his wand levelled, but Minsk was much faster. She spat two short, sharp bursts of energy, and with a hiss and a puff of smoke, the figures crumpled and vanished.

"Anymore for anymore?" Minsk asked, in a tone that wasn't playing.

Larch's grip tightened around my throat momentarily before his eyes flicked over to Ezra. The tension grew unbearable and I shuddered, but then Larch's hand slackened, dropping away from my neck. I stumbled back, catching my breath. "Who were those people?" I wheezed.

"Just a couple of grubby underworld assassins," Minsk said. "Nothing to worry about."

"Certainly no need for violence," said Ezra, his voice rising while maintaining his air of calm. "Friends of yours?" he asked Larch.

Larch shook his head. "You'll get nothing from me."

"We're only trying to fathom out the truth," Ezra said.

Larch glared at him, then at me before retreating to his seat, sinking down and putting his head in his hands. My heart pounded in my ears, but I nodded gratefully at Ezra, moving closer to Minsk—what a warrior she was—and putting some distance between myself and Larch.

"Alright," Minsk said, breaking the silence. "Back to the matter at hand. We all know Plunge was set up, so why don't you tell us how?"

"I can't," Larch moaned, his voice muffled. "Do you think I want to spend eternity burning in the fires of everlasting hell?"

"Work with me and I can get you to a safe place," Minsk offered.

"There *is* no safe place," Larch said, and it sounded to me as though he were weeping.

I massaged my neck. I'd be bruised in the morning. "Come clean," I begged. "Salve your conscience."

Minsk nodded. "A full and frank confession might go *some* way to helping the situation ..."

Larch's head dropped forward, his hands falling between his knees. "All I can tell you is that ... I succumbed to ... pressure ... to throw the case."

"*Who* was pressuring you?" Minsk pressed.

Larch shuddered. "I can't tell you that."

"The *actual* murderer?" Ezra asked.

"No, no, no!" Larch frowned. "I have *no* idea who the murderer was, I swear. We— I ... never properly investigated. It was ... suggested ... to me that I find ... a scapegoat."

"And Murgatroyde Plunge?" I asked.

"Was convenient. She knew the children, she'd been with them before they disappeared. It was easy to pin it on her."

I clenched my fists. "But she was innocent! You ruined her life!"

Larch nodded, not looking at me. "For that I'm sorry. But I had no choice."

"What about Greta?" I asked. "Murgatroyde was

charged with her murder even though her remains were never found."

Larch locked his jaw, thinking. He shrugged. "Again, we—I—concocted charges, but—"

"But?" I demanded, refusing to let it drop.

"I— I ..." Larch's reluctance was more obvious than ever. "I don't believe that Greta was killed in the burial place."

"Then what happened to her?"

Larch held his tongue.

"You won't tell us?" I asked.

"I don't know what became of her." He shrugged.

"What about markings in the graveyard? Did you see any symbols anywhere?"

Larch pressed his lips together, looking through me.

"Was it you who sent people after me?" I asked. "Did you have someone break into my house?"

He regarded me with sudden interest. "A break-in? What do you have that someone else might want?"

Now it was my turn to clam up.

Larch levelled me with a gaze. "You need to be careful," he hissed. "Very careful. Sounds to me like you're in danger."

Ezra spoke up. "Who is she in danger from?"

Larch refused to answer.

"Will you tell us who ordered you to do all this?" Ezra asked.

Larch hesitated.

Around us, the shadows seemed more fluid than previously. Unnerved, I whipped around, brandishing my ridiculous wand, but neither Minsk nor Ezra seemed concerned.

Larch appeared to be battling with some internal conflict, but the arrival of these new shadows suddenly spurred him into making a decision. He sighed deeply. "What can I tell you? Who ordered me? My boss? His boss? All the way up to the mayor?" he whispered.

"Tumble Town's mayor?" Ezra asked.

"I don't know for absolute certain!" Larch cried. "And I would never be able to prove it, but that's what I believed at the time. I was told—and I won't give you names—that the mayor needed the case closed quickly to avoid a scandal that could ruin his political career."

The revelation hung like a dark cloud, heavy with implications. The betrayal ran deeper than any of us had imagined. I could feel the weight of the truth pressing down on us all.

Minsk was the first to break the silence. "Were you asked to fabricate the truth in other cases?"

After an interminable pause, Larch nodded. He appeared smaller now, a man crushed by his own actions. There was no more time for regret. The shadows around us shifted.

"Alright, Greenbalm," Minsk called, and three cloaked figures stepped into the light.

"Sarge?" one of them asked.

"Arrest him," Minsk ordered.

"What's the charge?"

"We'll start with misconduct in a public office and take it from there," Minsk decided.

Two of the figures moved towards Larch, wands drawn. The pair worked together to quickly and efficiently draw a criss-cross of energy around him, while Greenbalm stood before Larch to read him his rights. I watched, flabbergasted, as the criss-cross became a cage of energy that could prevent the escape of any ghost.

I swiped at a single tear that rolled down my cheek. "Poor Murgatroyde."

"We'll make it right," Minsk said quietly. "I'll let you know what happens." She turned to supervise the cloaked figures—members of her team, I supposed.

"Let's go," Ezra directed me, and I followed him up the stairs into the back room of the tavern, through the lounge, where Burly Man stood at the bar scowling, and back out into the street. I took a deep breath, glad to be in the fresh air, even if it was smoky, grimy, stinking Tumble Town air.

"I'll walk you home," said Ezra.

Home. That sounded good. "I could sleep for a week," I told him.

"When you're dead, you'll be able to," he said. "Works for me."

"I think I'll wait awhile before I put that to the test."

He laughed. "Speaking of testing, Wootton sent some photos over to your address."

"I thought he would text them."

"He figured you'd appreciate hard copies."

I nodded. "He managed to age Greta?" I'd forgotten about that.

"Yes, with all his software thingummies." Ezra waved a hand dismissively.

"How exciting!" I said. "I can't wait to see what he's come up with."

CHAPTER TWENTY-EIGHT

I probably should have returned to work the next morning, but I slept late and by the time I'd woken, showered, made myself a coffee and studied the photos Wootton had couriered over, I knew that broomstick permits would have to wait for another day.

After washing up, sweeping the kitchen floor—which didn't need doing—and staring in dismay at my empty bookshelves, eventually I realised there was a task I couldn't put off any longer.

I climbed the stairs of my apartment block to Flat 6, the photos and my grimoire tucked under my arm, and rapped on Mr Redhill's door. As soon as he cracked it open and spotted me standing there, his face fell.

I smiled to cover my nervousness. "How are you?" I asked.

"So, so." He hesitated. "I've been expecting you to come up here again ever since we first had our conversation about your grimoire."

I nodded, wondering whether he intended to send me away with a flea in my ear. Instead of doing that, he opened the door wide. "Come on in," he said. "Tea?"

"Please."

He directed me through into his living room and pottered around in his kitchen for a few minutes until the tea was ready. During the interim, I stared at his images of Glynis. There was no mistaking her resemblance to the photos I had in my possession. By the time Mr Redhill joined me, I'd spread my images out on his dining table—both the ones Wootton had sent me and a copy of Greta as a young girl at the time she went missing.

He deposited his tray beside them and reached out, hands trembling a little to smooth the likenesses. "I suppose you have questions," he asked.

"Lots of them," I replied, my tone gentle. "But I hardly know where to begin."

"Take a seat," he said, and I did so, placing the grimoire to my right. It might have been my imagination, but the book had an odd energy to it today. Impatience? I decided this was probably a reflection of how I was feeling.

"Greta and Glynis were one and the same?" I asked.

He nodded. "They were. Yes, they were." He absently smoothed the image of Greta as a child. "I didn't know. Not until after we'd married." He reached behind to take his wedding photo off the wall. Him looking thin and bashful but smart in dark robes, Glynis—or Greta, I supposed—in a beautiful 1920s-style wedding dress, with shoulder-length hair. "Not that it mattered. I loved her. I love her still."

"Of course." I wasn't here to take any of that away from him. I cleared my throat. "Not that it's any of my business, but ..."

"You want me to tell you her story." Mr Redhill's forehead creased.

"The authorities know that Murgatroyde had nothing to do with the children's disappearance," I told him. "The Dark Squad are looking into obtaining a pardon for her."

I was surprised when Mr Redhill's eyes filled with tears. "Oh!" He lay a hand over his heart. "Glynis would have been so pleased to hear that. It was a constant weight on her mind that someone innocent had been sent to prison over her brother's death."

"And hers," I reminded him. "Murgatroyde was committed for both murders."

"True." Mr Redhill collected himself and began pouring the tea. "Glynis didn't divulge much information about what happened, but she remained a troubled soul her whole life."

"Tell me what you know," I encouraged him.

He nodded, handing me a cup and saucer. "Okay."

I waited. Mr Redhill shuddered before finally beginning to speak. "Glynis was always a little cagey about her background. She told me her mother had died while she was young and that she and her brother were sent to a series of care homes in and around Tumble Town."

I sipped my tea. This much I knew.

"She also told me her brother had died young but for a long time didn't share the details. And that was fine with me. It was her prerogative."

"Yes."

"After we'd been married a few years, I discovered that work wanted to send me abroad. Incredibly exciting! I expected Glynis to be thrilled, but she quite obviously wasn't. Her unease became apparent when she needed a passport. For that, the authorities required her birth certificate."

"Of course."

"She became extremely agitated. I'd never seen her so anxious. When I pressed her about it, she finally told me everything. She couldn't apply for a copy of her birth certificate because that would have her birth name on it."

"She didn't want to be found?" I asked.

"Never. Not by *anyone*. She'd left her early life far behind her."

I chewed my lip. It sounded more and more like Glynis—or Greta—had a guilty secret. I fully expected Mr Redhill to confess to me that his wife had indeed killed her brother.

He didn't.

"You see, Zilla ..." Mr Redhill took a deep breath. "Glynis told me that she and her brother were witnesses to a crime *a week before he was killed*."

"Witnesses?" I frowned. "What sort of crime?"

"Murder."

Wow. This was getting deeper. "Who?"

Mr Redhill raised his palms. "You have to understand she never gave me any names. She was paranoid that someone would come after her—and me if she told me. I think she had suspicions about the victim but she never talked about it."

"And she knew who did it?" My hand stroked the bruises on my throat.

"Again, she never divulged any names, but she always said she would recognise him anywhere."

"Did she go to the police?" I asked.

"She told her foster mother, who invited the police to speak to her, but this was Tumble Town and no-one followed it up. Except—"

"Except?"

"Two nights later she was visited in the foster home by someone who claimed he was from the police. This man told her and her brother that they needed to keep their mouths shut, otherwise they'd end up at the bottom of the Thames."

"Oh boy." Threatening children? The lowest of the low. "They must have been terrified!"

Mr Redhill nodded. "She certainly understood he meant business, whoever he was."

"Did she ever mention seeing this person again?" I pressed further.

"No."

"Or the murderer?"

"No. But four nights later, she and Socrates were

ambushed as they walked home, and Socrates was killed."

The whole thing stank of a cover-up. After everything that Larch had told us the night before, it struck me that I'd opened a proper can of worms.

"How did Greta—Glynis—get away?"

"She said she fought, she broke free and ran. She knew the streets well. She evaded them."

"And she couldn't go back to the care home," I said. They would know where to find her.

"Exactly. She lived rough for a while. Disappeared deep into Tumble Town. That's easy enough to do. Eventually she built herself a whole new identity."

"Crikey." I sat back in my seat, my tea forgotten. "And she remained scared for the rest of her life?"

"Oh, yes," Mr Redhill said, his voice broken. "Suffered constantly with nightmares. Don't get me wrong, she had moments of happiness—joy even—but they were always tempered by what had happened to her brother and what might happen to her. Or me. It's why we never had children. She didn't want to put any other lives at risk."

"I am so sorry," I said, my eyes filling with tears. "If only someone could have helped her."

Without warning, the cover of my grimoire flung

itself open, slapping the table. We both regarded it in surprise. The pages full of writing and illustrations—the flowers and butterflies, grass and bees and dandelion seeds exploding into the air—flipped faster and faster and faster until finally reaching a blank page and settling.

I reached out and lay my palm on the page, warming it, willing it to tell me what to do. Nothing happened. It was almost as if it was waiting for me to decide ...

On a whim, I pushed it closer to Mr Redhill. "Put your hands on the pages," I said. "Next to mine."

He humoured me, tears on his cheeks. The pages vibrated and his eyes widened.

The tingle ran from my fingertips up my arms ... and suddenly I knew. Murgatroyde had wanted her name cleared, but she would also have wanted justice for those two children she'd been so fond of—seven-year-old Socrates who loved making models, and eleven-year-old Greta who had adored her brother.

The grimoire waited expectantly.

What choice did I have?

"I'll do it," I said. "I'll find out who murdered Socrates and who ruined Greta's life."

The grimoire shimmered, the two uppermost pages beginning to turn from off-white to a buttery cream. *Yes. Yes. Yes.* Black ink ran across the left-hand side. *Yes. Yes. Yes.* On the adjacent page, a rectangle, sketched in pencil, gradually emerged as if being drawn by an unseen hand. The sides were rapidly and realistically shaded and started to rise from the surface of the paper, revealing an envelope. Letters materialised, one by one, slightly higgledy-piggledy as though typed on a vintage typewriter. I angled my head to read what was written there.

The last will and testament of Murgatroyde Plunge.

EPILOGUE

Standing in the front room of Murgatroyde's dwelling, I surveyed all I could see with a grimace.

"It's all yours," the lawyer had said when he'd handed me the keys this morning, but now, as I scanned the boarded-up shop window and door, the muck and dust and broken glass, I wasn't even sure I wanted it.

"Nothing that a dustpan and brush won't clear up," said Humphrey, opening up the step ladders he was lending me so we could put some bulbs into the light fixtures. He'd been thrilled to find out Murgatroyde's final will—written while she was in prison—had left everything to me, naming me specifically, even though she couldn't have known me from

Adam. Another case of predictory magick, Dodo had said when I'd taken the will to Wonderland Detective Agency.

"A dustpan and brush, an enormous skip, a serious quantity of supplies from a DIY megamarket, half a dozen builders, carpenters, painters and decorators, not to mention a plumber and an electrician and—"

"A bit of elbow grease." Humphrey smacked his hands together. "Let's get stuck in."

I didn't have the heart to tell Humphrey I was considering selling the old place. It would take me years and years to be able to afford the work that needed doing here. Working for the Ministry of Witches wasn't lucrative enough. Instead, I turned to Blue. He was picking his way through the shards of glass covering the wooden floorboards. "Watch your paws," I said.

"Why? What are they going to do?" Blue asked, regarding them with studied solemnity.

"Don't cut yourself!"

"Why would I want to cut myself?" Blue asked, leaping nimbly onto the step ladders and from there to one of the shelves. "Ooh! Shiny things!"

"Mebbe you ain't so allergic to cats after all," Humphrey observed.

"It's a spell," I confessed. "Blue has enchanted me so I can tolerate him."

"Ain't that kind?" said Humphrey approvingly.

"I need an additional enchantment to tolerate his attitude, but so far he hasn't offered me one of those," I grouched.

"Shiny! Shiny!" called Blue. I could hear things scattering around on the top shelf and hoped nothing was about to die up there.

Humphrey handed me a broom. "Will you use this shop as a shop?" he asked. "Or turn it into a front room? I sees that's what some folks does."

"I'd love to use it as a shop," I said, moving to the corner nearest the door with the broom preparing to sweep. "It would be a dream come true to have my own retail premises, but I don't have the capital to do anything like that." I thought of the mauve notebook with the research I'd started, my scruffy handwriting lopping over the pages in different coloured pens.

"Is *anyone* interested in my shiny things?" Blue called down, a little put out that we were ignoring him.

"What sorta shop?" Humphrey pressed.

"A bookshop," I said. "I always wanted a book-shop." This conversation put me in mind of the one I'd had with Lionel. That had only been a few weeks ago, but how my life had changed since then. I'd solved a mystery, made a new best friend in Humphrey, inherited a dwelling all of my own and adopted a cat. Or been adopted by a cat, I wasn't quite sure.

In turn, that reminded me of Lionel's token. I lay the broom aside and located my purse. The token was in the middle section. I fished it out. Even in the dull light, I could see it trying its best to sparkle.

"An arcanologist needs a shop of arcane tomes," said Blue, his sweet, furry face peering down at me from his perch high above my head.

"I'll bear that in mind," I said, "as I sit at my desk issuing permits all day long for the rest of my sad and sorry life."

"Never give up on yer dreams," said Humphrey.

"They'll come true quicker than you think," Blue assured me.

I regarded Blue suspiciously. "You haven't stolen another grimoire, have you?"

He peered over the shelf, whiskers twitching. "Would I?"

"I don't know ... would you?"

He blinked at me, all wide eyes and innocence. "You haven't completed the to-do list in *your* grimoire yet."

"Mmm." I hadn't forgotten. Well, I sort of had. *What was it? The spookiest of the spooks? The somethingist of the—*

"Catch!" Blue shouted down.

A flash of green rolled off his shelf and plummeted towards me.

"Wah!" I ducked, but at the same time instinct took over. With the token in my right hand, I reached for the object with my left and, by some miracle, actually caught it. The weight of it took me by surprise. It was a cut-glass jar in emerald green with a silver stopper, about the height of my thumb. It appeared to be vintage. I pulled the stopper out and peeped inside. Empty.

"Pretty," I said and, without thinking, popped the token in the jar, replaced the stopper and positioned it on a shelf behind where—in my head—I imagined a shop counter would go.

You never know, I thought. *One day ...*

NEED MORE GHASTLY GRIMOIRES?

The Spookiest of Spooks: Ghastly Grimoire Mysteries Book 2

"All eyes on you!"

Zilla Chaplin is unnerved.

And so would you be if you were being pursued by voices in the shadows who insist on whispering vague warnings. "You're being watched", "Being followed!" "Being targeted!" ... and not by these sinister, invisible nobodies, but by something far, far darker.

Zilla isn't entirely surprised. After all, she recently

became the keeper of a grimoire that helped her solve a small part of an historic murder mystery.

But now it seems the grimoire has more secrets to spill ...

This is a tad worrying for Zilla because she's good at issuing broomstick permits but not a lot else. Fortunately—or unfortunately, depending on whether you like big-headed, smug, ridiculously fluffy cats or not—Zilla can enlist the help of Blue, her untrusty familiar, to assist her.

Are either of them prepared to come face to face with the most malevolent ghost who ever stalked the afterlife?

Zilla's not so sure. Her ghastly grimoire however, has other ideas!

Available for pre-order now.

ALSO BY JEANNIE WYCHERLEY

The Complete Wonky Inn Series

(in chronological reading order)

The Wonkiest Witch: Wonky Inn Book 1

The Ghosts of Wonky Inn: Wonky Inn Book 2

Weird Wedding at Wonky Inn: Wonky Inn Book 3

The Witch Who Killed Christmas: Wonky Inn Christmas Special

Fearful Fortunes and Terrible Tarot: Wonky Inn Book 4

The Mystery of the Marsh Malaise: Wonky Inn Book 5

The Mysterious Mr Wylie: Wonky Inn Book 6

The Great Witchy Cake Off: Wonky Inn Book 7

Vengeful Vampire at Wonky Inn: Wonky Inn Book 8

Witching in a Winter Wonkyland: A Wonky Inn Christmas Cozy Special

A Gaggle of Ghastly Grandmamas: Wonky Inn Book 9

Magic, Murder and a Movie Star: Wonky Inn Book 10

O' Witchy Town of Whittlecombe: A Wonky Inn Christmas Cozy Special

Judge, Jury and Jailhouse Rockcakes: Wonky Inn Book 11

A Midsummer Night's Wonky: Wonky Inn Book 12

Halloween Heebie-Geebies: Wonky Inn Book 13

Owl I want for Witchmas is Hoo: A Wonky Inn Christmas Cozy Mystery

Oh Mummy!: Wonky Inn Book 14

Pieces of Hate: Wonky Inn Book 15

The Faery of Witchmas Past: A Wonky Inn Christmas Cozy Special

Wonkytonk Witch: Wonky Inn Book 16

A Wonky Apprentice: Wonky Inn Book 17

A Barbarous Band of Blood Brothers: Wonky Inn Book 18

The Witchy Wood and the Weirdly Wyse: Wonky Inn Book 19

By All That's Green: Wonky Inn Book 20 (to be released September 2025)

Spellbound Hound

(*in reading order*)

Ain't Nothing but a Pound Dog: Spellbound Hound Magic and Mystery Book 1

A Curse, a Coven and a Canine: Spellbound Hound Magic and Mystery Book 2

Bark Side of the Moon: Spellbound Hound Magic and Mystery Book 3

Master of Puppies: Spellbound Hound Magic and Mystery Book 4

Dem Bones, Dem Bones: Spellbound Hound Magic and Mystery Book 5

Born to be Styled: Spellbound Hound Magic and Mystery Book 6

Up, Pup and Away: Spellbound Hound Magic and Mystery Book 7

Another One Bites the Crust: Spellbound Hound Magic and Mystery Book 8

Grimly Fiendish: Spellbound Hound Magic and Mystery Book 9 (to be released May 2025)

Wonderland Detective Agency

Dead as a Dodo: Wonderland Detective Agency Book 1

The Rabbit Hole Murders: Wonderland Detective Agency Book 2

Tweedledumb and Tweedledie: Wonderland Detective Agency Book 3

The Curious Incident at the Pig and Pepper: Wonderland Detective Agency Book 4

A Tragic Tea Party: Wonderland Detective Agency Book 5

The Pool of Tears: Wonderland Detective Agency Book 6

Into the Labyrinth: Wonderland Detective Agency Book 7 (Release TBC)

The Municipality of Lost Souls

Midnight Garden: The Extra Ordinary World Novella Series Book 1

Beyond the Veil

Crone

A Concerto for the Dead and Dying

Deadly Encounters: A collection of short stories

Keepers of the Flame: A love story

With Peter Alderson Sharp

The Creature from the Grim Mire: A humorous Sci-fi, Time Travel and Alien Contact Mystery

Non-Fiction

Losing my best Friend

Thoughtful support for those affected by dog bereavement or pet loss

Follow Jeannie Wycherley

Buy me a coffee

www.buymeacoffee.com/jeanniewych

Find out more at on the website

www.jeanniewycherley.co.uk

Or visit her on Facebook for her fiction

www.facebook.com/jeanniewycherley

Follow Jeannie on Instagram (for bears and books)

www.instagram.com/jeanniewycherley

See Jeannie on Tiktok @jeanniewycherley

Sign up for Jeannie's newsletter on her website

www.subscribepage.com/JeannieWycherleyWonky

Printed in Dunstable, United Kingdom

74523288R00201